Take Me Down

CARLY PHILLIPS

Opposites not only attract, they combust!

Parker Knight was going through the motions… and then he met her.

In sweet, sexy Emily Stevens and the rundown resort she runs with her father, Parker sees the chance to reclaim the life he once lost and take care of the first woman who makes him feel … everything. He wants her in a way he's never desired a woman before and yearns to sample the treats the sexy baker has to offer.

But Emily doesn't trust charming city guys, especially one who is going to leave when his time off is over. No matter how good he makes her feel, in bed or out.

Parker has his hands full, not only with a wary Emily but with someone who doesn't want the lodge to succeed, and if things keep getting worse, not even a Knight can save her.

Chapter One

"HEY, HANDSOME." THE pretty barista with green eyes and light brown hair leaned over the counter, giving Parker Knight a good glimpse of her ample breasts, peeking out from the deep vee of her black shirt.

Pity his dick wasn't interested.

"What can I get for you today?" she asked, wriggling her eyebrows, obviously offering more than coffee.

Behind him, his brother Sebastian snickered.

"I'll take a medium dark roast," Parker said, ignoring his sibling.

As he ordered coffee only, silently declining her proposition, she flashed him a disappointed smile and turned around to make his drink.

"Come on, she's cute," Sebastian said as they walked to the counter where they would pick up their cups. "She looks about your age, she's obviously into you. Would it kill you to give her the time of day?"

Parker shook his head. "I'm not interested and it

wouldn't be fair to her to make her think otherwise."

Sebastian groaned. "Then who are you interested in? Because in the last couple of years, I can count on one hand the number of women you've been with."

"Says the one-time player," he muttered under his breath. "I didn't know you were keeping track of my sex life." With a roll of his eyes, Parker turned his attention to his phone, checking email until his name was called.

When he picked up his coffee, he noticed the phone number handwritten onto the cup and groaned.

Still laughing as they exited the shop, Sebastian turned to him. "Ready to meet with Ethan?"

Parker paused. "Not really." Considering his oldest sibling, the one who ran their company, had been a raging asshole lately, why would Parker want to deal with him?

Granted, Ethan had his reasons. It had only been eight months since Ethan's wife, Mandy, had passed away from an accidental overdose, and since then they'd discovered that not only had she been abusing drugs and cheating on Ethan, she'd also been stealing from the company to finance her habit. Ethan had taken the news hard and he was no longer the same person he'd once been. True, he'd never been Mr. Happy-Go-Lucky, but he'd never been quite the pain in the ass he was now.

"I hear you," Sebastian said. "But it's not like we have a choice, so let's go. He called the meeting for nine a.m."

A short while later, Parker and Sebastian had joined Ethan and their sister, Sierra, the company's social media coordinator, in Ethan's office.

Ethan sat behind his large mahogany desk, glaring at them as they entered. "You're late."

Sebastian glanced at his watch. "It's a minute after. Calm your shit," he muttered.

Parker glanced at his oldest sibling. As usual these days, Ethan's appearance was a shock. He looked nothing like the man who used to come to the office, hair cut short and maintained monthly, expensive suits and ties befitting the executive he was. Now? His hair was long, overgrown ... much like Parker's had been in his skiing days, and he didn't always wear a suit to work. Hell, sometimes he looked like he'd pulled out the first thing he'd laid eyes on in his closet and dressed.

"Come on, man, can't you at least get a haircut?" The words were out before Parker could censor them.

Sebastian chuckled.

Sierra hid a grin behind her hand, which had a big-ass diamond on it along with her wedding band, having gotten married a few months ago to Sebastian's best friend, Ryder Hammond.

3

"Bite me," Ethan muttered with a scowl. Parker couldn't tell if the look was due to his haircut comment or the fact that this had become his permanent resting dick face.

In another lifetime, Ethan would have laughed at the comment. For Parker, it was easier to joke than face the truth. Ethan looked exhausted and Parker's heart squeezed in his chest, feeling bad for his brother.

"Sierra and I already went over a few social media concerns that I had. Sebastian, you have Keystone under control?"

"No issues," Sebastian said.

Knight Time Technology supplied high-tech security for smart buildings and state-of-the-art corporate parks, and Keystone was a multimillion-dollar defense contractor establishing a new, secure headquarters in northern California. The same project Ethan's now deceased wife had nearly lost for them because she'd been working with the supplier, using substandard material and pocketing the difference so she could support her drug habit.

The owner, Stephan Romano, had given them a chance to fix the problems, and when they'd come through, thanks to Sebastian, he'd given Knight Time Technology the contract on other corporate headquarters he was building, as well.

"Good. Parker." Ethan met his gaze. "I need you

to go to Denver to scope out a place for our annual corporate retreat. We're going to the mountains this year. Jenna had an appointment to tour the lodge and see its amenities but she was rushed into emergency gall bladder surgery so she can't make it. I know it's not your normal job but we could use someone with the knowledge of ski resorts to make a decision. That's you."

The order – not, he noticed, a request – took him off guard. Parker wasn't the scout for corporate retreats and his brother damn well knew it.

In fact, Parker hadn't been back to the slopes since he'd been hurt during the qualifying trials for the Olympics, shattering his knee and destroying any hope for the Games that year. He'd competed four years before, when he'd been eighteen, and had two bronze medals to show for it. Four years later came the injury, then surgery and nine months of rehab and he'd returned to the sport, only to be sidelined by a car accident that had broken his leg, again taking him out of competition.

An accident that had caused more than damage to Parker's body. Given everything that had transpired that day, he'd been emotionally and physically broken. He hadn't had it in him to qualify against much younger skiers another four years later and was forced to let his dreams and hope for the future go. The thought of returning to the mountains was emotionally terrifying.

"Hey, man. I can take the flight out and handle it," Sebastian said, shooting Ethan a narrow-eyed glare. If Ethan was too self-absorbed to realize what he was asking of Parker, Sebastian wasn't.

"I can do it," Parker said, ignoring his churning stomach. Facing his fears wasn't necessarily a bad thing.

"If you're sure…" Sebastian trailed off.

"I am."

Sierra rose and placed a hand on his shoulder, squeezing once. She also understood that what Ethan was asking wasn't as simple a request as it sounded.

Ethan cleared his throat. "You and Sebastian can go. I need a word alone with Parker."

Sierra frowned at Ethan. "I think *you* need the vacation," she said to him. "Your mood sucks." Without waiting for an answer, she spun on her heel and walked out.

Sebastian turned to his oldest sibling. "She's got a point, bro. We've been patient but you need to check the attitude and fix yourself. Even I've fucking had it." He walked out the way Sierra had gone, leaving Parker alone with Ethan.

"What is it?" Parker asked. He had more patience for Ethan's moods because he knew what it was like to have his entire world shattered.

"The accountant red flagged certain transactions coming out of your personal account." Ethan picked up a folder from his desk, holding it in his hand.

Anger stirred in Parker's gut. "Why didn't Ashley bring this to me instead of you?" Ashley, Sebastian's wife – they'd married in a small, family-only ceremony a few months ago – was a forensic accountant who had come back into their lives and later their business – after nearly a decade and was now working with Knight Time Technology.

"It wasn't Ashley who flagged the payments. It was Frank at our outside firm. And he couldn't reach you. Thought I'd just relay the information."

Parker swallowed hard. At least his family wasn't betraying him. "It's none of your business, Ethan." He curled his hands into tight fists. The thought of his oldest sibling, who'd been like a father to him, knowing his failures wasn't a good one.

Ethan ran a hand through his overlong hair. "You're my brother. What affects you affects me. And this?" He pointed to the folder, which, Parker knew without looking, listed payments he had made to the London family.

Large payments.

Guilt money.

"It has to stop," Ethan said.

7

Parker shook his head, the pain of that time returning full force. "Their daughter died, Ethan. I owe them."

Ethan's expression turned angry. "That's how they want you to feel. You were driving the car but you were broadsided by another vehicle. It wasn't your fault and you have to quit acting like it was."

Parker pinched the bridge of his nose and groaned. "I hear you. I may even agree with you but they need the money. Between their mortgage, Rina's student loans, and her medical bills from the time of the accident until she died, they're in serious debt."

Ethan shook the papers in his hand. "Wrong. First, if someone dies, the student loans are discharged. Second, they had decent insurance, and third ... they're not using the money on anything remotely resembling helping their family. Read the private investigator's report." He held out the file.

Pissed now, Parker snatched it from his brother's hand. "You had no right to go digging into what I do with my money."

Ethan raised an eyebrow, not at all concerned that he'd gone looking into things that didn't concern him. "Family," he said, as if that explained his actions.

Parker opened the folder and began reading through, and what he saw turned his stomach. High-end cars, vacations abroad, shopping at expensive stores, private school for their other child … basically the Londons were living a life of luxury on his dime. Or Benjamins, as the case might be.

"I've tried to say no once before but Elana, Rina's mother, cried about how hard their life was without her, how much money they owed. George, her father, acted like he hated coming to me at all but it was a last resort… Even if they've been using the money for frivolous things, their daughter is gone. I'm not. I owe them."

Rina had been his college girlfriend, his best friend, the woman he thought he would be spending the rest of his life with until she'd been killed in the car accident that had ended his chances at the career that had been mapped out for him since he'd started skiing at five years old.

Ethan placed a hand on his shoulder. "I'm sorry. They've been taking advantage of your guilt – survivor's guilt – and using the fact that you have money to profit off their daughter's death. But you don't have to pay it, Parker."

"Is this why you're sending me to scout locations? So you can handle this for me? Because I'm an adult. I can make my own decisions just fine."

"I know that. I really do need you to handle finding the perfect place for the retreat. Who knows mountain resorts better than you?"

Parker allowed himself to relax. Ethan wasn't trying to undermine him. Just to take care of him in his overprotective way.

"Fine on the retreat, but as far as the payments, it's my choice to make."

Ethan's scowl merely deepened. Parker knew it wasn't because his brother hadn't gotten his way but because he didn't agree with Parker's choices. Well, tough. Ethan didn't have to live with the guilt. Parker did.

THE SIGHT OF the snow on the Colorado mountains soothed Parker's soul in a way he hadn't experienced since his life's passion had been taken away from him. Even the fact that he'd hated the place he'd gone to scope out for the company's next corporate event didn't bother him in the least. The so-called lodge had been more like a ski resort, all chrome and white, too sterile, too much luxury for Parker's liking. He preferred rustic wood and fireplaces. He'd find something else. Eventually.

Instead of heading home, he decided to take another day or two and drive around, get his fill of the back roads and snowy mountains.

He had a room at the Ritz-Carlton booked for tonight in Denver but had driven three hours to the resort he'd hated, then spent the afternoon touring back roads in the rental car, enjoying the scenery and the peace of mind he found here.

He drove on until his rental car started driving weirdly and he didn't want to end up stranded on the side of the road. He pulled into the nearest gas station he came upon. The only one in the small town of Montlake, Colorado, according to the sign that greeted him.

A man about his age came out to meet him wearing coveralls. He had grease on his hands and had obviously been working on a car when Parker had pulled in.

"How can I help you?" he asked.

"Car's acting odd. I'm afraid of getting stuck if I drive any farther."

The other man wiped his hands on a rag and nodded. "Drive it into the bay and let me take a look." He gestured to the large garage with room for his car.

While the man checked it over, Parker sat in the small office, going through email on his phone. The amount of busywork that accumulated while he was away was staggering, and he called his assistant, letting her know he expected her to handle things while he was gone. He'd been training her for a while now and she was more than capable of taking the reins. He didn't want to deal with bullshit while he was away.

He fucking hated the paperwork and dealing with clients that came with his job. He'd never intended to be a behind-the-desk guy. Hell, he'd never thought beyond his skiing career, yet he'd known it would have ended sooner or later, but by then he'd have had a plan. Forced retirement at twenty-two hadn't been on his agenda. Yeah, he'd managed to finish college while skiing, Ethan would have kicked his ass otherwise, but it wasn't until he'd retired from the sports scene that he'd gone to school for his MBA and into the family business.

The mechanic returned, coming into the office through a door that led to the garage. "I'm sorry to tell you there's a problem with the axle. It's not safe to drive and needs a new part."

"It's a rental," Parker muttered.

"And there's nothing nearby. You can call the rental company and look into how they want to proceed or I can order the part. Regardless, it's going to be a few days, I can guarantee you that from experience."

"Fuck." Parker ran a hand through his hair, in no mood to deal with the company and their telephone representatives. "Tell you what. Order the part and I'll handle the rest on my end later on today. In the meantime, can you recommend somewhere for me to stay that's nearby?"

The man rubbed a hand over his bearded face. "The only place close is the Ruby Rose Inn. It's a bed-and-breakfast about a mile down the road."

"Do you think they'll have a room?"

He sighed. "They've got one foot in the grave, so to speak. The place isn't really up and running but I'm sure they won't turn you away since they have the space. Tell you what. I'll drive you up the road with your things and you can see what Emily and her dad can do for you."

"What about the station?" Parker gestured to the pumps and the open garage bays.

The other man shrugged. "I'll lock the doors. Besides, I'll only be gone five minutes max. Guaranteed I won't miss anyone."

Small-town living, Parker assumed. "Thanks. I appreciate the ride…"

"Matt. Matt Banks," he said, holding out his hand for a shake.

"Thanks, Matt. Parker." None of that Mr. Knight bullshit was necessary for him.

He grabbed his suitcase from the trunk of the car and let the other man drive him to the aptly named Ruby Rose Inn. The wood-framed structure was painted a deep red with white trim and snow covered the surrounding bushes and grass. But the closer he got, the more he realized that the outside looked as if it had seen better days. The paint was chipping and the roof was old.

But at least it had a roof, he thought, as Matt pulled the car to a stop.

"If you have a problem, give me a call and I'll come back to get you. Though I can't see Emily turning you away. She's a sweetheart," he said, a look of longing in his gaze as he spoke of the woman who owned the inn.

There was a story there, Parker thought. Or Matt wanted there to be one.

"You coming in?" Parker asked as he opened the door and climbed out.

"Wish I could but I can't leave the place unattended for that long. Tell Emily I said hi."

"Will do." Parker retrieved his suitcase from the back. "Thanks for the ride."

He looked up at the inn and hoped like hell the owners took pity on him and gave him a room for the night.

✧　✧　✧

"MEN SUCK." EMILY Stevens pounded the dough for the bread she was making for her dad and glanced up at her best friend, Harper Sanders.

"Did the asshole call again?" Harper raised an eyebrow, a talent she'd always had and Emily envied.

"He did. I'm thinking of changing my number except he knows where to find me, so what good would it do?" She shivered at the prospect of seeing her ex-husband again. She never knew when the bastard would show up to harass her.

"You could file for a restraining order."

She looked at her friend through lowered lashes. Where Emily was thin … but for the tummy pooch she still had, Harper was curvy. Where Emily was blonde, Harper was dark haired. And gorgeous. And her best friend in the entire world, bar none. They'd been inseparable until Emily moved to Chicago to try her hand in the big city. The city … and the man she'd met there had all been a mistake.

"I can't prove emotional abuse and you know it," Emily reminded her friend. "I just have to hope Rex gets the hint and moves on." To some other unsuspecting woman who thought he was the amazing man he appeared to be on the surface.

She'd moved back home and away from the son of a bitch almost a year ago. She'd filed a petition of separation and had to live apart from him for one more year before the divorce would become final in the state of Illinois, where they'd married and lived. Unless he came to his senses and didn't contest the damned thing. So far he was ignoring the fact that she wanted out, showing up on occasion to pretend he

15

was a misunderstood great guy who wanted his wife back.

She knew better.

Hell, *he* knew better.

He was a lawyer who didn't like to lose, and by her walking out, he considered that a loss. Being rid of him in any way, she considered a win.

Emily wanted the life she had now – living in her small town, baking for Harper's Coffee Shop, and lying low.

"Look, we can talk to my brother. Gary's your lawyer and you know he'll help you," Harper said.

Emily shook her head. "He already told me the process is playing out. He said to document any bad behavior, but other than that, Rex calling me or coming by isn't harassment."

Harper pulled on her long black hair and groaned. "I call bullshit. I'm going to talk to Gary."

Since Harper was stubborn, Emily didn't argue. "I'm through with the opposite sex." Had been for longer than she'd been separated, in fact. But there was no use dwelling on things she couldn't change … or bring back to life.

She shaped the bread and slid it onto the tray and into the oven before turning back to her friend. "No more men," she said one last time for good measure.

"How's your dad?" Harper asked, ignoring Emily's

comment.

Harper was still trying to fix her up with people – not an easy feat in their small town where Emily knew everyone, thank goodness. Harper even gritted her teeth and pretended she was okay with Emily going out on another date with Matt Banks.

He asked her fairly often, as Emily was in town every day since she brought her baked goods to Harper's Coffee Shop on a daily basis and he owned the gas station and repair shop across the street. Problem was, Harper had had a thing for Matt since forever and the man was oblivious. Emily's first and only date with the man had been before she'd known Harper liked him that way.

"Dad's good," Emily said. "Still ignoring me when I try to talk him into moving to Florida." Near her sister, Amy, and her family. "It'll be good for him to stop worrying about this place. It's a money pit." She loved her dad and wanted him around for a long time to come, not worrying himself to death about how he could make this place succeed and fulfill her mom's dream. "Anyway, the winter is almost over, so I have the spring and summer to convince him to move there by next fall before the weather turns brutal again.

"Do you really want him to leave you here alone?" Harper asked.

Emily shook her head, a lump in her throat. "But I

worry about him and the memories here as well as the cold, the hard work…" Ever since losing her mom, she was ultrasensitive and worried about her father.

"I get it. I really do. But you won't be able to stay here if he leaves. He'll have to sell and–"

"I'll rent a place. Somewhere with a kitchen so I can still supply you with baked goods–"

"Hello?" a male voice called out from the front entryway.

"Are you expecting anyone?" Harper asked.

Emily shook her head. "Dad didn't mention anyone coming by, either." But they did occasionally get people who needed a room who would stop by. And they let them stay although they never operated at full capacity. There were too many fixes and problems that needed taking care of before they could be a full-fledged B and B. They just didn't have the money for the repairs they needed.

"Coming!" Emily yelled out. She wiped her hands on the apron she'd tied around her body, protecting her clothes, and headed out to the main part of the house, where people would congregate … if they were a fully functional bed-and-breakfast.

Emily walked into the room and came to a stop, Harper barreling into her from behind.

A man stood in the doorway, suitcase at his feet. From the designer shoes with the Gucci buckle to the obviously expensive jeans to the shearling-lined jacket, everything about him screamed city slicker. Just like Rex.

Her gaze came to his revealing blue eyes in a drop-dead gorgeous face, strong jaw, full lips, and distinctively handsome features. But his good looks didn't erase the fact that he was everything she'd come to distrust in a man.

"Can I help you?" she asked coolly.

He met her gaze with a friendly one of his own. "I'm looking to rent a room."

"I'm sorry but we're not open for business."

"Yeah, Matt mentioned something about that but–"

"You came here anyway, hoping to charm me into giving you a place to stay," she said as if it were a crime.

"Hey!" Harper nudged her in the back. "No need to be rude to the man. He's hot." She whispered the last part in Emily's ear.

He narrowed his gaze, probably not understanding her chilly tone. "Actually my car broke down and it needs a part. Matt has to order it and I need a place to stay while I call the rental place and figure out what happens next."

"No." Emily was adamant. This sexy, good-looking man wasn't staying in the room next to hers.

"But you're the only inn within hours and I'm shit

out of luck if you don't help me. Please." He treated her to what she supposed would be a panty-melting grin that worked on any woman who hadn't been subjected to a con man's charm before. She didn't trust his good looks or smile.

"Emily–" This from Harper behind her.

"Hey, darling daughter of mine. What's going on?" Emily's father joined them, walking down the stairs from where his bedroom was located. Emily's large room and the other guest rooms were on the opposite side of the house.

James Stevens was in his late fifties, he was strong, fit, and he liked to do more than he should around the house. He and Emily looked nothing alike. She'd gotten her blonde hair from her mom, God rest her soul. Her dad had brown hair and a scruffy beard. And he loved having guests. The bed-and-breakfast had been her parents' dream – until her mother got sick and things fell apart during her illness.

"Mr.– Oh! We don't even know your name," Harper said. "His car broke down and he needs a room."

"I'm Parker Knight," he said, giving Harper a grateful wink. A wink that turned Emily's insides to mush, not that she'd let him know that.

"James Stevens, and this is my daughter, Emily. And her friend, Harper."

Harper, the traitor, treated him to a friendly wave.

Parker chuckled and grinned at her before turning back to the older man. Emily refused to admit what that wink – at her friend – did to her insides.

"Your daughter said you aren't renting. But I'm really in a bind." He appealed to her father instead of Emily, obviously because she'd already turned him down. "So can you make an exception? Please?"

Her father turned to her, a frown on his face. "Emily Ann Stevens, I'm disappointed in you. How could you turn away someone in need? You know we rent to a person or two at a time. We just can't handle a full house." He turned back to the man named Parker. "Of course you can stay. Emily, show the man to a room, please."

Her stomach cramped as she realized she wasn't going to win this battle. The hot city guy was here to stay. For a couple of days or more, she didn't know. As far as she was concerned, one day was one too many.

Chapter Two

PARKER FOLLOWED THE little spitfire who wanted nothing to do with him, as she led him through the house and to a set of stairs, his gaze on her ass the entire time. Two flour handprints stained her jean pockets, making him want to set his palms there and squeeze those cheeks until she moaned, which only served to accentuate the already hard problem in his pants.

"You're the only guest we have," she explained, glancing over her shoulder only to catch him staring at her rear end.

She scowled at him and came to a stop at a closed door. "You can put your bag in here. It's been cleaned but I need to make sure you have towels and everything else you'll need, so I'll be back."

She started to head past him, the warm scent that followed her making his mouth water as he caught her wrist. "Why does having me here piss you off so much?"

The second he'd laid eyes on the blonde-haired,

brown-eyed beauty staring at him with a frown on her pretty face, hair up in a messy bun, and a *Kiss the Cook* full apron, he was intrigued both by her looks, a combination of wholesome and sexy, and the obvious animosity she had without even knowing him.

She pulled her bottom lip into her mouth before releasing it with a pop. "You look like trouble, city boy."

"Do you always judge a book by its cover?" he couldn't help but ask.

She didn't look the least bit apologetic for being called out on her behavior. "I don't, actually, but something about you has my gut screaming to watch out." She shook her head, glancing down at her small wrist, which he still had in his hand.

He immediately released her, missing the heat she'd generated in his palm. "Hey, I'm a nice guy. Some people even think I'm charming."

"That's what I'm afraid of," she muttered and he narrowed his gaze. He wondered what she had against him being from the city. Why calling himself charming put her off. And most of all, why, despite the fact that she had obvious walls around her a mile high, he wanted to climb them anyway.

"I'll be back up with fresh towels, some water, and a few other things."

"You don't need to wait on me. I can come down

and get them for myself."

"And have my father tell me I'm depriving you of the full Ruby Rose experience? No, thank you."

Okay, so he'd let her treat him like a guest. Which brought up another question. "Why aren't you open for business?" he asked.

Her heartfelt sigh went straight to his gut. "It's a long story."

"If the part for my car takes a while, like Matt said it would, I'll have time to listen."

She muttered something under her breath, turned, and walked away.

Chuckling, he rolled his suitcase in and looked around. Instead of a floral bed-and-breakfast appearance, it was a rustic vision of wood furniture and bed frame, accentuated by deeper red tones in the comforter and window treatment, and he loved the room on sight.

If he had to be stranded in the Colorado mountains, he could think of a lot worse places to be. One thing he knew for sure, he looked forward to getting under Emily Stevens' skin a whole lot more.

PARKER WOKE UP freezing. His body was shaking, his nose was cold, and his dick was shriveled. A glance at his watch told him it wasn't even five thirty a.m.

"Jesus," he muttered, climbing out of bed. He pulled on a pair of sweats and sweatshirt, went to the bathroom in the hall to take care of business, and made his way downstairs.

He heard the distinct sound of metal banging on metal from an open door leading to the basement downstairs. Curses followed and he went in the direction of the noise, finding James, wrench in hand, wrestling with the boiler.

"Come on, you son of a bitch. I can't afford what a plumber will cost me to come fix you," the man muttered.

"What's going on?" Parker knelt down beside James, who was also bundled in jeans and a heavy jacket. "Damn thing is old. I think I'm going to have to call for help."

Parker wasn't good with machinery and groaned. "Sorry. I wish I had the know-how to help."

They both rose to their feet.

"It's fine," James said with a wince. "I'll give Timmons a call. He's the plumber in the area. Hopefully he can get out here fairly soon. I'm sorry about this."

"No worries for me. Let's go have some hot coffee," Parker said, gesturing toward the stairs for them to walk up.

A little while later, he and James were sitting at the table while he waited for a return call from the plumber, each cupping their hand over a warm mug of brew.

"I'm sorry my daughter wasn't exactly warm and welcoming yesterday," James said. "I'm not sure what got into her."

Parker chuckled. "I think I just rubbed her the wrong way."

Although he got the feeling there was more to her dislike of him than met the eye. Between her calling him city boy and thinking he was trouble, he figured maybe he reminded her of someone she knew and didn't like. He'd have to give it more time. From his check-in with Matt a little while ago, the part would take a few days, and Parker had decided he was in no rush to return home. In fact, he felt as though he could breathe here without feeling suffocated by work and family issues.

"She's been through a lot," James said of his daughter. "Don't hold it against her."

"I won't," Parker assured the man. He was too interested in the attraction he felt for Emily to do that. "What's going on with the heater? Is that typical?"

James sighed, meeting his gaze. He looked to be in his late fifties, with deep creases around his eyes that came from living life, and Parker wondered what his story was.

"Emily grew up in this town. It's small and slow-paced. Her mom and I loved it here. I was an accountant and her mother was a stay-at-home mom. It was always my wife Ruby's dream to open a bed-and-breakfast and we saved for that day. Emily went off to college and then settled in Chicago, and her mom and I waited for the perfect property to come up for sale. Five years ago, it did." He stared wistfully off into space, as if remembering.

"And you bought it," Parker said, bringing his attention back to the present.

"We did. And it needed a lot of work, which we started to put into it. But that didn't stop Ruby from living her dream and getting guests here to stay over. She loved taking care of people and she loved being the proprietor. We did the renovations slowly even with a small loan. But then…"

He trailed off and Parker waited for him to be able to continue.

He glanced from his mug into Parker's eyes. "Ruby got sick. Pancreatic cancer. And when the treatments didn't work, the money we'd allotted for the inn we started to use for experimental treatments. This place was the last thing I worried about and I let things go."

"How long has she been gone?" Parker asked softly.

"A year." He blew out a harsh breath. "It wasn't easy. Emily came home as often as she could, when that bastard would let her." He muttered the last part under his breath, and Parker narrowed his gaze, not liking what his words insinuated. At all.

"Finally she returned for good and her mom passed a short time after. Which is why we don't have the money to get this place fixed up so we can accommodate a full house of guests."

Parker nodded in understanding, taking a sip of his coffee before answering. "I'm very sorry for your loss."

He knew both personally and from his brother what death did to people, and it was a wonder they had this place running even at partial capacity.

"I want more than anything to fulfill my wife's dream, but in the meantime, Em is baking and selling her cakes and cookies at Harper's Coffee Shop in town. It's a good fit since she left her job in Chicago when–"

"Dad!" Emily's bark of horror stopped her father from finishing his sentence, preventing Parker from learning more.

Which was fine with him. Anything about Emily, he intended to learn from the woman herself.

"We were just discussing the heat," Parker said.

"Is the boiler out again? I woke up freezing." She held up her hands, which were covered by fingerless gloves.

She was bundled in a pair of leggings, a long

sweater, and a scarf wrapped around her neck. Her hair was once again pulled into a messy bun, and she had on no makeup, which didn't detract from her beauty. She was naturally pretty, so unlike the women he met on a daily basis in Manhattan. He couldn't help but be struck by her looks ... and prickly personality that was obviously a cover for something that had happened in her life.

Color him curious.

"I have a call into Timmons Heating and AC. He'll get back to me."

She nodded. "Soon, I hope. I can't move my fingers but I wanted to be able to make coffee and start my baking, so I didn't put on my full gloves."

Parker rose to his feet, headed for the cabinet where he'd seen James pull mugs from before, and proceeded to take one out and pour Emily a cup of coffee. "Milk and sugar?" he asked.

James was watching them carefully, something Emily must have realized because she put on a sweet but obviously fake smile. "Both, but I can get them myself. But thank you."

She made herself her coffee, pouring enough milk in to lighten it to the point where he cringed. Ditto on the sugar.

"What?" she asked, obviously catching his wince.

"Want a little coffee with your milk and sugar?"

"So I like it sweet. Shoot me."

He chuckled and took a sip of his own drink.

"Black?" she asked with a knowing grin.

He nodded. "One step short of mainlining my caffeine." He drank what was left in his cup, placed it down on the counter, met her gaze, and winked.

She blushed, a sexy shade of pink staining her cheeks. "Dad. Are you too cold? Do you want to go stay with Aunt Rhonda?"

James, who had been watching them with an interested look on his face, glanced at Parker. "My sister," he explained. "And no. I can handle the chill. I want to be here when Timmons arrives. I want a fix, not a whole new boiler, no matter what he tries to sell me. We can't afford the replacement right now."

Parker listened to the man's words, his mind whirling. He wanted to help them. They were good, hardworking people who deserved a break. And if anyone understood grief and heartbreak, it was him. But he sensed he had two proud individuals on his hands and they wouldn't accept a handout, no matter how easily he could afford to fix their boiler … and other things around the inn.

Especially Emily, who had distrusted him on sight.

He placed his mug down on the table and drew a deep breath. "Let's see what the repairman says before you go making any decisions. Sometimes repairing is only prolonging the issue, putting money in that could be put to better use."

"Says the rich man?" Emily asked, her tone one of utter disdain.

He shook his head. "Says the practicalities of the situation. It's obvious to me that this place means a lot to your dad. I'm just thinking of the best way to get it up and running the way he wants."

"I think we know what we can afford to do better than you." She slammed her mug down. "Dad, I need to start baking," she said, turning her back on him and taking items out of the pantry.

Parker followed her moves, his gaze on her ass, as was becoming his favorite pastime. But knowing her father was in the room, he jerked his head to the other man before he realized what Parker was up to. "Sorry to cause trouble."

James shook his head. "She's stubborn like her mom. She has it in her head that I'm too old to run this place by myself. I just need a plan, that's all. And for things to stop breaking so I can get ahead of myself."

"I can hear you," she reminded them.

James chuckled, as did Parker.

"Are you still doing taxes?" he asked the man.

"I got out of the business when we opened the inn and it's been five years. But I could start again. Take a few refresher courses online. It might help bringing in money here to fix things." He tapped his fingers on the counter in thought.

Parker nodded, his mind suddenly inundated with ideas to help them … that would do nothing but piss off Miss Emily. He needed to think through what kind and how much help he really wanted to offer. But he knew he *could* help. If they were willing to accept.

His cell phone, which had been sitting on the counter, rang and Ethan's name flashed on the screen. "Excuse me," he said to James and answered the phone. "Hello."

"How'd the tour of the lodge go?" Ethan asked.

"Hi, Ethan. I'm fine. How are you?" Parker muttered. "The tour went fine if you like a cold, sterile, too slick and packaged environment."

"I'm sure we could make it work. Jenna liked what they'd offered on the phone."

"And you sent me to check the place out and make a decision. I decided it won't work for us."

"Fine," Ethan bit out. "What options do we have then?"

"I'm not sure," he admitted. "I'll do some research when I get back." He glanced out the window in the family room, where he'd retreated to in order to take the call. The sun shone on the green grass, and in the distance, snowcapped mountains dotted the horizon.

Colorado was a gorgeous place.

"When are you home?" Ethan asked.

"My rental broke down so I'm stranded for a day or so. I'll get in touch when I'm back in Denver." And before his brother could rant or argue, Parker disconnected the call.

Broken-down rental or not, he had no intention of rushing home any time soon.

EMILY DROVE INTO town in her car, an old Jeep she'd bought when she moved back home. She delivered her baked goods to Harper and stayed for a cup of coffee with her friend. Her shop was a gathering place in town, had a regular breakfast crowd, and Emily knew everyone by name and the same in return. Harper had hung bright-colored pictures of cups and mugs on the wooden walls, and around the shop were shelves of homemade items created by local artisans that were for sale. One of the ways this town thrived was by friends helping and supporting each other.

After the morning rush ended, Harper carried two lattes over to the table where Emily sat waiting and joined her. "Whew. That was crazy. But your muffins are gone. The banana ones sell like hotcakes. Bake some more for tomorrow?"

"You got it." Emily loved that people enjoyed her

muffins, bread, cookies, and cakes, things she loved making so much more than the perfect petit fours she'd been forced to craft working at the high-end pastry shop in Chicago. She was a small-town girl at heart and she liked what she liked.

Too bad she hadn't listened to her own needs when she'd been with Rex, who, despite the fact that she was baking for a living when he met her, encouraged her to make better use of her culinary background than working for an Italian bakery owned by a husband-and-wife team. In truth, he wanted to be able to say his wife was a pastry chef, not a baker. Why had he gotten involved with her in the first place? Because he liked molding women into the dutiful female who made him her sole focus to the exclusion of everything and everyone else that made her who she was.

"Have you given any thought to going into partnership with me?" Harper asked. "The space next door is still empty and we could enlarge the shop, put in a kitchen where you could bake without having to take over the counters and oven at the inn. It would really be awesome, don't you think?"

Her heart began beating harder in her chest. Had she given it thought? Yes. A lot. Did she think she could abandon her father and the inn to do it? No. Besides, what made her think the bank would give her a loan? She was on the verge of divorce with very little to her name.

"God, Harper. I'd love to but I have to worry about my dad and the inn. If he closes it down and moves to Florida with my sister, then I can think about my own dreams."

"You know, having the inn booked solid would mean more people shopping in town. A rotating group of people coming in on a weekly basis. We just need to figure out a way to get the money to do both."

Emily glanced at her untouched drink. "Dad's maxed out. He owes so much money, nobody will lend him any to fix up the inn, and as for me, if I go to the bank for a loan, it's iffy they'll give me one. And if they do, I need to help my dad."

Harper sighed. "I understand. I'll keep thinking. The landlord promised not to rush into anything with another renter until he gives me the opportunity first. Nobody's come to him as far as I know."

"Okay," Emily said, sad because she knew how much expanding meant to Harper. But without Emily's baking, there was no reason to take over the expense of a larger place or the renovation it would entail.

"So … on another subject, how are things going with your newest guest?" Harper asked.

Her best friend could peg Emily's type, and the

stranger with the beautiful blue eyes and sexy grin was it. Too bad she was over men. Especially the kind she knew were bad for her. Luckily between the fact that he'd turned in early and the heater being out this morning necessitating them all bundling up, she hadn't had a visual of him without a heavy jacket or sweatshirt. No hint of whatever muscles lay beneath all the clothing.

Which was a good thing. Although she had a bathroom in her room, he didn't, which meant there was a good possibility she'd pass him in the hall on the way to or from the shower. Her body came alive at the possibility, despite the fact that the man wouldn't roam the halls naked.

"He's fine," Emily muttered, because her friend wouldn't give up until she got an answer.

"Fine." Harper drummed her fingertips on the table, clearly not satisfied with the one-word answer.

Emily nodded. And Harper stared her down, wanting her to elaborate.

"You know you're a pain in the ass, right?"

Harper chuckled. "That's my job as your best friend."

Emily covered her face with her hands. "Okay! He's sexy, all right? Those blue eyes, strong jaw, and full, kissable lips."

Harper glanced behind her, eyes suddenly wide.

"Kissable, huh?" a familiar male voice asked.

Shit and shit, Emily thought, blushing hard as she met Parker's grin. As embarrassed as she was, she wouldn't let him get to her or think she liked him. "He's also nosey, frustrating, and arrogant," she added for good measure.

Parker burst out laughing and the genuine sound went straight through her. "I can't say you're the only one to call me the last two but nosey? Now that's a first."

Without asking permission, he pulled out the chair beside her, turned it backwards, and sat down, joining them.

"Make yourself comfortable," Emily muttered.

It was warmer today than it had been yesterday, and wherever he was from, he'd obviously prepared for the variable Colorado weather. Warm one day, below freezing the next. He wore a hunter-green Henley shirt, the three buttons on the flat collar open, revealing a smattering of dark chest hair. The fit of the shirt showed her muscles she'd been wondering if he possessed, definition that could only be gotten at the gym. She swallowed a groan at the fact that not only was he hot, he had a great body, too.

"How did you get into town?" she asked, knowing his car was in for repair across the street.

"Your father lent me his truck. He needed a few

things from the hardware store and I picked them up for him before coming in here."

"Well, it's good to see you," Harper said. "Can I get you a coffee? On the house?" She smiled at Parker, disloyal bitch that she was.

"I'd love a cup. Black is good."

Harper jumped up. "I'll be back."

Emily knew her friend was matchmaking and would inevitably take her time, and she wanted to strangle her.

"Too much caffeine isn't good for you," Emily said to Parker, wrapping her hands around the cooled cup of coffee.

"Then it's a good thing I didn't finish mine this morning. So how did your sales go today?" he asked, sounding truly interested.

After the boiler had been fixed – luckily it hadn't been anything horrendously expensive – the heat had kicked back on, making her baking easier. He'd gone to shower and returned as she was finishing, packing her items to bring into town. He'd insisted on helping her, carrying her packed and covered baked goods out to the car and loading up the trunk.

"We had a good morning. Banana muffins sold out," she said with pride.

"Cool. I'll have to get one tomorrow before that happens."

"You'll still be here tomorrow?" she asked.

He nodded. "I called Matt this morning and he's waiting for a ship date."

"You could … you know, arrange for a ride back to wherever you came from?" She raised her eyebrows at him hopefully.

Taking her by surprise, he rose, flipped the chair, and sat down again, this time leaning close. "But what kind of vacation would that be? I like this small town, the proximity to the mountains, and I'm relaxed for the first time in … forever. So I figured what's the rush?"

She blinked at him in surprise. He wasn't leaving any time soon?

"Besides, your father said he has no problem with me staying. And I can help him with some things around the lodge."

She unclenched her jaw enough to say, "Swell."

She glanced around enough to know they were still alone. Harper was in the back, stalling in her making of a basic cup of coffee.

"Look," she said, leaning forward, too close to the man. He smelled good, woodsy, musky, manly, she thought, doing her best not to squirm in her seat. "You might think the lodge is a fun project while you're here and taking a break from whatever you're running from at home, but this is our lives."

40

"I respect that, Emily," he said, his tone serious.

"Then respect the fact that my father doesn't need you feeding him hope about the lodge. It's falling apart, we don't have the money to fix it, and he needs to go live with my sister in Florida, where he can take it easy and enjoy life. I'm this close to convincing him." She elaborated on her words by gesturing with her thumb and forefinger. "So please, for the love of God, don't give him hope we really don't have."

He stared at her for so long she grew uncomfortable. There was something going on behind those piercing blue eyes and she couldn't figure out what it was. And that made her nervous. She couldn't deny the attraction between them was mutual. He was an extremely good-looking man and she'd be lying if she said otherwise. But the last thing she needed was another overly confident male in her life who swooped in and thought he knew what was best.

Time to put him on the defensive, she thought. "So what are you avoiding back home, city boy?"

Those clear eyes shuttered quickly, confirming her suspicions. He had problems and secrets of his own.

"Not so interested in me digging into your issues, now are you? I'll make you a deal."

He reached across the table and slid a strand of hair that had fallen out of her ponytail off her face, his fingertips trailing over her cheek, leaving goose bumps

41

in their wake. In fact, he woke up parts of her that had gone dead and dormant after Rex had gotten through with her. Her nipples pebbled beneath her shirt and awareness tingled between her thighs.

"What did you have in mind?" he asked, taking her thoughts off of the things he did to her body, but the physical remnants of her need remained.

"You stay out of my family's business and I'll stay out of yours."

"Coffee!" Harper said, returning with his cup before he could respond.

Emily took that as her cue to leave. "I need to get going. It was ... interesting talking to you, Parker." She rose to her feet. "Bye, Harper."

"But—"

"Talk to you later!" she trilled. Having had the last word, she headed for the door in order to escape.

Except when she got to her car and turned on the ignition, it chugged and chugged and didn't come to life.

"So much for a grand exit." She put her head in her hands on the wheel and groaned.

✦   ✦   ✦

"STRUCK OUT?" HARPER asked Parker as she sank into the seat Emily had vacated seconds before.

"I don't know what you're talking about," he lied.

It was obvious to anyone within a twelve-foot radius of him and Emily that there was some serious chemistry arcing between them.

Harper laughed.

He glanced at the gorgeous brunette who, with her voluptuous curves and easy disposition, was exactly his type. So why did he find himself attracted instead to the willowy blonde determined to keep him at arm's length?

"Don't pay her any mind. She's been through a lot in the last few years. She's wary of strangers."

More like she was wary of something about the kind of man she thought him to be. But he wouldn't push her friend for answers.

"Are you the type to give up easily?" Harper asked him.

He appreciated her directness. "Not a chance in hell," he said with a grin.

"Good. Just one thing."

Parker tipped his head. "Yes?"

"Hurt her and I'll make the Lorena Bobbitt story sound like a fairy tale."

He winced and had to physically stop himself from cupping his dick in his hands. Still, he admired the loyalty and protectiveness of the women's friendship.

He glanced out the window only to see Emily climb out of her car and kick the wheel with her foot.

He narrowed his gaze and was rising from his seat before he could think it through.

"I take it you aren't going to be drinking that?" Harper asked, chuckling.

"Sorry. Rain check?" he asked, sliding his hand into his pants for his wallet.

She waved her hand through the air. "Don't worry about it. I told you it was on the house. Go help her," she said, her gaze falling on Emily through the window. "Trust me, you'll want to get there before Matt does."

"He's interested?" he asked, not surprised based on the look in the man's eyes when he'd dropped Parker off at the inn yesterday.

"And persistent."

Parker caught something in Harper's voice and glanced up in time to see disappointment in her gaze. "You like Matt?"

"Does it matter? He's got a thing for my best friend."

"His loss," Parker assured her.

She smiled. "Thanks."

Taking Harper's words to heart, though, he rushed out of the coffee shop and onto the street.

He walked up to Emily mid-curse. "Problem?"

"My car won't start." She glared at the vehicle. The navy Jeep looked well maintained on the outside but it

44

was obviously old.

"Does it give you a hard time often?" he asked.

"Not really. I baby it. Living here, I don't go long distances. I just need to be able to navigate in any kind of weather. I didn't need a brand-new car, just a reliable one."

"Tell you what. Why don't we go across the street to Matt, leave him the keys, and I'll drive you home?"

This way he could stake a claim of his own on this unpredictable woman and let Matt know if she hadn't said yes before now, she wouldn't be agreeing to date him any time in the near future.

Chapter Three

O F ALL THE luck. Emily's jeep died and the man she was actively trying to avoid because of how much she desired him was walking her across the street to the man who was constantly trying to get her to go on a second date.

She'd only gone on the first one because her father had insisted she get out of the house and he'd done so in front of Matt after he'd asked her to go for dinner. He was a nice guy. They'd gone to school together, had known each other forever, and she enjoyed his company. But she wasn't sexually attracted to him and she wasn't looking for a relationship. Two reasons to avoid sending him the wrong message. Harper liking him made him completely off-limits.

Parker was silent as they made their way across the street and walked into the office of Matt's garage, but she felt his presence beside her every step of the way.

"Hello?" she called out and Matt immediately walked in from the bay area.

"Hey, beautiful."

She did her best not to cringe at the endearment. Or blush. Or acknowledge it at all. "Hi, Matt. My car died." She gestured to the vehicle parked on the street in front of Harper's.

His gaze swept from her to Parker, who he acknowledged with a nod.

Arms folded across his chest, Parker returned the gesture.

Matt glanced out the window as he wiped his hands on a rag, then tucked it into his back pocket. As he did, she couldn't help but take in the differences between the men. They were both extremely good-looking, both had dark hair, a scruff of beard, and blue eyes. Similar on the surface, but that was all.

The women in town thought Matt was a catch and she agreed. He was well-built, down-to-earth, and rugged in a mountain-man sort of way. If she were looking for a guy, Matt and his laid-back personality was exactly the type she ought to go for. He was nonthreatening to her way of life and what she needed for a peaceful existence. He liked her for who she was and had never tried to change her. The direct opposite of her soon-to-be ex-husband. A man with an imposing presence like Parker had.

Yet it was Parker and his leaner-yet-still-fit body that did it for her. Parker, whose scruff was lighter and more refined, who lit her body up and made her wonder what that facial hair would feel like against her skin, chafing at her thighs. Parker, with his take-charge personality that signaled trouble, that turned her on.

Dammit, this so wasn't fair.

"Em? I asked if you have the keys for me?" Matt said, breaking into her unwanted thoughts.

"Oh, sure." She pulled the key chain from the purse hanging on her shoulder and handed them to him.

"I can take a look while you wait," he said.

"No," Parker said, obviously deciding for her. "I'm going to take her home. You can call the inn later and let her know what's wrong. I can bring her back to pick up the car then." He grasped her elbow, causing a frisson of heat and awareness to sizzle up her arm, making her way too aware of the demanding man by her side.

Matt's gaze settled on where Parker touched her, his eyes narrowed. "About that dinner we talked about?" he asked her, pushing when she'd been putting him off and trying to be nice about it without having to reject him outright.

Apparently it was time for her to explain to him she only liked him as a friend. But she couldn't do that in front of Parker. That would only serve to humiliate the man, and she couldn't do it to him. Nor did he deserve to be treated in that way.

"How about dinner? Friday night?" Matt asked.

Parker's hand on her arm squeezed tighter. He wasn't hurting her, rather it was a possessive hold. And though she knew she'd been emotionally beaten down by her ex, he'd never threatened her physically and Parker's actions didn't scare her.

Annoy her? Yes. Arouse her thanks to his nearness and the manly smell of him so close to her? Yep, that, too.

She turned her focus to Matt, uncomfortable but knowing she had to deal with the situation once and for all. Harper would appreciate her letting him down gently, and if she happened to put in a good word for her friend and try to open Matt's eyes ... even better.

"Umm ... okay," she said.

No sooner had she spoken than Parker pulled her toward the exit.

"I'll call you about your car," Matt said, either clueless to Parker's reaction or not caring.

Parker pushed open the door and they walked onto the street, his big body vibrating with something she couldn't quite name, heading straight for her father's truck, which she hadn't noticed parked around the corner.

He walked quickly and she stumbled to keep up.

"Hey! Slow down!" she said, shaking her arm loose. "What is wrong with you?"

He moderated his pace, waiting until they reached the truck before he turned, bracketing her against the side of the vehicle with his hands. "You're going on a date."

She narrowed her gaze. "Yes."

"No. You're not."

"You don't get to tell me what to do, Parker. I've had enough of that with— I mean I'm an adult. I can do what I want." She had no intention of getting into personal details with a man who wasn't acting particularly rational.

Although she couldn't say she minded the fact that he was jealous… It was flattering in its own way. But she was wary of any guy who told her what she could or couldn't do. Rex was good at that, and though she'd found it sexy at first, she'd quickly realized it was in his nature to control everything, not just about their relationship but about her, as well.

Parker met her gaze, tipped his head, bringing himself nose to nose with her. "Maybe I should rephrase. I don't want you to go on a date with Matt."

"Except it's not your decision to make." And the fact that he thought it was made her want to defy him just because she could.

"Unless I change your mind," he said in a husky, growl-like voice.

She swallowed hard. "You can try." And a naughty

part of her hoped he did.

"Hmm." The sound reverberated in long-neglected places, causing a distinct tingling between her legs and making her nipples tighten in need.

She swallowed hard. And then his lips came down on hers. She gasped at the shock, despite having sensed it was coming, and immediately opened for him, meeting him more than halfway, willing in spite of herself. In spite of the fact that he represented things she didn't want in her life or for herself. Because she wanted him.

He slid his hands through her hair, his palms holding her face, tilting her to the side so he could glide deeper inside her mouth.

She moaned at the delicious invasion, her tongue dueling with his, the kiss turning hot fast despite the fact that they were outside. He aligned his body with hers, chest to chest, his thick erection nudging unmistakably against the rising heat between her thighs.

More. She needed more. But before she could reach for it, he broke the kiss and stepped back, putting unwanted distance between them. At least, until she came back to herself and realized the error she'd just made both in action and in judgment.

"Still going on that date?" he asked, his tone too smug for his own good.

"Damn right I am," she muttered, and because

he'd been such an arrogant ass, she refused to enlighten him about the date being a means to explain to Matt that she wasn't interested. Let Parker Knight stew while she was out with another man. It would serve his arrogant ass right, she thought, turning to stomp away.

"Emily, I'm your ride home," Parker called out with a chuckle.

Dammit. Cheeks burning, she turned back around, making her way to the truck, only to find him waiting with her door open. Like a gentleman.

Too bad he was anything but.

PARKER SAT ACROSS the dinner table from James Stevens, eating the older man's delicious stew. According to him, it was his wife's recipe and he fed it to all guests sometime when they stayed at the inn. He admired the man's dedication to the love of his life and his determination to keep her spirit alive.

James was the opposite of his daughter, open where she was closed off, warm and friendly where she was snippy and wary. But he saw now, a part of why she was so prickly was because she'd lost her mother, an obviously strong presence in both James' and Emily's lives. But he sensed there was something deeper that kept her wary and apart from people in her life. From men specifically. And Parker in particular.

Although she'd let her guard down during that kiss, and holy hell, had it been spectacular. He discreetly adjusted his dick under the table at the thought of how hot she'd been in his arms.

Unfortunately, he'd also been in the kitchen when Emily had bounced down the stairs for her date. She hadn't been dressed up. She didn't need to be in order to knock him on his ass. Tight jeans tucked into a pair of high boots that made her legs look long and lean and he wanted them wrapped around his hips as he sank his cock deep inside her. Her blouse revealed a hint of cleavage, not enough to give Matt any wrong ideas, but if Parker was imagining those small globes in his hands, the asshole would, as well. He frowned at that.

She'd kissed her dad on the cheek, told them not to wait up, just as a car honked from the driveaway. Parker had looked up in disbelief.

"Classy," he'd muttered, not under his breath. Even her father had chuckled. And with a look that promised retribution, she'd walked out the door to where Matt waited inside his warm truck.

"Did Matt call to say what's wrong with the car?" Because he still didn't have an estimated time on Parker's rental, not that he cared. He could have called for a car and left here at any time. He wasn't ready to do that, though.

James shook his head. "I assume he'll tell her to-night."

Parker scowled at the reminder of her date.

"I see that face you made," James said, assessing him. "Can't say I think he's the right man for my girl, either. But I can see why she'd give him a shot."

Parker raised his eyebrows.

"I won't spill secrets, but since I've seen how you look at her and how she treats you in return, I wanted to explain a few things."

He didn't deny his interest in Emily. That would make him a liar. As long as her father wasn't violating any confidences, Parker wanted to hear. "Go on."

"Just know that her last relationship was with a man who didn't deserve her. And he had a thing for telling her what to do, when to do it, and most importantly, he wanted to change who she wanted to be. So if you fell in here, saw a pretty girl, and decided you'd have a little fun, you can shut those thoughts off right now. My daughter has been used and manipulated enough."

Beneath the table, his hands curled into fists at the thought of anyone trying to change the woman he was just coming to know. He didn't know what made her tick or why she responded to him the way she did. But he knew he liked what he saw and not just the physical responses, although those were a damned good start.

He appreciated that she didn't take his shit. She told him off when she felt like it. And now he had an inkling as to why. Because something about him reminded her of her ex and not in a good way. He stored away the little bit of ammunition her father had provided to take out and dissect later, so he could figure out how to break down Emily's steep walls.

Leaning forward in his seat, he met her father's gaze. "I didn't have a father who cared like you obviously do and I'm glad your daughter has that."

He didn't like to think about Alexander Knight, who abdicated the parental role to his eldest son, focused instead on his company and the rotating women who came and went in his life after Parker's mom died from cancer as he'd begun middle school. He remembered her, though, and knew she'd loved them all, had been there for them, and would have hated what their father had become and how he treated his kids.

Parker cleared his throat. "And I respect the fact that you're letting me know how you feel. The truth is, I came here by accident but I'm staying because I want to. I feel a pull here, something that is making me want to stay." The inn, the mountains, and the woman. It was a combination of all those things. "And the last thing I'll do is play games with your daughter." It was the best he could offer the man, given that he'd just met Emily yesterday and had already kissed her once. Not that her father needed to know that.

James studied him, taking his measure, then he obviously decided he liked what he saw because he nodded. "I think she's out with Matt because he's nonthreatening. There's no way she's interested in him and Matt just doesn't want to realize it."

"I noticed that."

Social cues weren't Matt's forte, because he'd completely ignored Parker's possessive hand on Emily's elbow and the scowl he'd shot Matt's way. Of course, if he'd looked out his garage office window after they'd left, he'd have seen Parker and Emily setting the street on fire with their kiss.

"So about the inn," Parker said, changing the subject. "Emily wants you to sell. What do you want?"

James, who wasn't an old man by any stretch of the imagination, might not be capable of manual labor, but he was more than able to take care of people who came here for a weekend, assuming he had the right kind of help.

"My daughter worries too much. She wants me in Florida like I'm an old man. If she had her way, I'd be covered in bubble wrap." He laughed but the sound was pained. "Losing her mother hurt us both. Losing…" He cut off whatever he'd been about to say.

"She's worried about me. But I can handle the work, despite what she believes. What I don't have is the capital to fix what needs repair. Everything about this place is old, from the boiler to the roof. If I'm going to give guests a good experience, it needs to be done all at once. It doesn't help to have a pot filling with water on a rainy day in a guest room."

Parker shook his head in understanding. "No, it doesn't."

James drummed his fingers on the tabletop. "I haven't told Emily, but I've gotten pressure from a big corporation to sell and it's for good money."

Parker narrowed his gaze. "But?" He picked up on the other man's reluctance.

"This is a small town. We pride ourselves on our identity. If I sell to a conglomerate, they're going to build a slick, high-end resort. It'll put the little guy out of business. Harper's Coffee? It'll become a Starbucks. The Corner Store? A Target or Walmart. Or worse, some upscale store nobody who lives here can afford. I don't want to be responsible for that kind of destruction." He shook his head. "No way, no how. But I know Emily will see it as my way out. It'd hurt her to hurt her town, her friends, but if she thinks it'll keep me around longer? She'll push for it."

"James, are you sick?" Parker couldn't help but ask.

The man shook his lightly graying head. "No. But we both learned cancer doesn't discriminate and she's a scared little girl inside. So I haven't told her about the offer."

Parker got it. And despite the fact that lying never sat well with him, he understood why James was withholding the information from his daughter.

"On the other hand, if I can get this place up and running with a full house on a regular basis, especially in season, all the smaller businesses would profit from the tourists spending money in town. Not to mention how much this place meant to my wife. It was our dream. I want it to live on. I want to leave it to my daughter one day."

As he listened to James' explanation, the wheels in Parker's head began to turn and excitement filled him for the first time in forever. He could do this. Help them, both financially and with the physical labor necessary on smaller fixes. It'd been a long time since he felt useful. Yeah, he worked for the family business but Ethan didn't need him. It was more a place to park his ass when everything else had fallen apart.

He needed enjoyment in his life. Excitement. To feel like he was making a difference. And, he realized, he could do that here.

"I'll tell you what," he said to James. "I'll front you the money." He knew better than to say he'd just outright pay for it. The man had pride and Parker wouldn't step on it. "And I'll stick around to help fix things for as long as it takes."

James' mouth opened and closed in obvious surprise.

As if sensing the enormity of the moment, Parker's cell rang. He'd changed Ethan's ring so he'd recognize if he wanted to avoid his brother's call. "Sorry," he said to James. "It's my oldest brother."

"Take it," James said. "I'm going to start cleaning."

Parker knew he had to face the music sooner or later at home and he figured the man needed time to think and consider his offer.

He answered the phone, helping James clear the table at the same time. "Hi, Ethan."

"Parker. Any news on the rental?" Ethan asked.

"No but—"

"Just call a car service and get your ass home. We have a new account I want you to take over," his brother said.

Parker frowned, no thrill coming to him over the thought of another smart lock account to handle. "Listen. I'm taking a vacation."

"What?" his brother all but barked in surprise.

"A vacation? You know, days off? The kind I haven't taken in at least three years?" Because he hadn't wanted downtime to think about what he'd lost or what he no longer had to look forward to. "I'm due."

"Parker, what's going on?" Ethan asked, sounding like the concerned older brother he used to be and not the ass who'd been duped by his drug-using, now-deceased wife.

He bit the inside of his cheek. "I need this time for me, Ethan. I'm staying." And with that, he disconnected the call.

Drawing a deep breath, he turned to face Emily's dad. "So what do you say? Will you let me help?"

"With a real contract and provisions for payback?" James asked.

"Yes."

"And you'll stay on here free. I'll cover room and board while you're here."

Parker didn't like it but he sensed it was a deal breaker. It wasn't easy for a man to admit he couldn't afford to solve his own problems, let alone take money from … a city slicker, he thought wryly.

"Deal," he said, extending his hand.

He and James shook hands, sealing their agreement. Then they finished cleaning the kitchen in silence, each alone with their thoughts, James' probably on saving his beloved inn, Parker's back on Emily and when the hell she would be back from her date.

After they finished cleaning, James went upstairs to read, leaving Parker alone in the family room with a fire in the fireplace, a glass of bourbon in his hand, and his thoughts, which grew darker the longer Emily was out with Matt.

He sat in a chair facing the front with a good view of the driveway and tilted his head back in thought. When was the last time a woman had him twisted up in knots? He could answer in one word. Never.

Rina had been his high school best friend. They'd had skiing in common and drifted into a relationship. He'd loved her for sure. Cheated on her never. Hell, she'd been his first and only, until awhile after her death. But theirs had been an easy relationship, no highs and lows, no crazy fights or minor bickering.

Which brought him to Emily. In a short span of time, she'd taken an immediate dislike to him, which had translated into hot sexual tension the likes of which he'd never experienced. She'd gotten under his skin. So he was sitting in her father's chair, waiting for her to come home from a date, his fingers itching to spank her for daring to go out with another man.

Based on what her father had told him about her last relationship, that wouldn't go over well at all. Still, he wasn't going to roll over and be a doormat like Matt, letting her call all the shots when he knew their sparring made her hot.

Which left him waiting ... and wondering how he should handle her when she returned.

✧   ✧   ✧

EMILY WAS HANGRY. Her steak had been tough and she hadn't sent it back, always feeling badly for the chef when she did. It hadn't helped that Matt seemed to love his sirloin, devouring it quickly. If she'd asked to have her order redone, by the time she got her food, he would have been finished with his meal.

And she'd have had to spend more time listening to him expound on his love of cars. He talked about engines. Carburetors. Things she'd never heard of, didn't care about, and never wanted to learn. Of course she'd like to hear about his business, but this went beyond. Into the realm of boring and oblivious to the fact that her mind was elsewhere.

On another man and the kiss he'd given her that had rocked her world and scared her to death. The last thing she wanted to do was make another mistake, choosing a man who was all wrong for her, a lesson she'd learned all too well with Rex. Who did he think he was, telling her she couldn't go out on a date? She didn't need or want another controlling guy. But it was clear, sitting across from Matt, that passive wasn't doing it for her.

What made matters even worse was the fact that he'd chosen a restaurant where the tables were close together and she hadn't been able to have the private talk she'd wanted, which meant she'd have to do it when he pulled into her driveway.

The weather had changed while they were inside and it had started to rain. She wanted to talk quickly so she could run inside before the light drizzle became a downpour.

Finally, he made the turn into the inn's drive and parked not nearly close enough to the house for her to get inside easily without getting drenched in the rain. She sighed.

"I had a great time tonight," he said, turning to her, his arm reaching perilously close to her as he stretched it over the back of the seats.

"It was lovely, but Matt, I need to talk to you."

He stiffened.

She rushed on. "I like you … as a friend. I hate to be cliché but it's not you, it's me. I'm not in a place for a relationship, and even if I were, I think we're too different." There, she'd said it, she thought, her empty stomach churning.

He hadn't even asked her if she wanted dessert, just requested a check after he'd finished his dinner.

"I hate that line," he muttered.

"I'm sorry. It's just that sometimes it's the hard truth. Thank you for dinner." She actually debated offering to pay for her meal again.

"You're welcome," he said sullenly, and she felt

bad. Rejection was never fun for anyone. And it certainly didn't feel like the time to bring up Harper as a possibility for him.

Knowing the best thing to do was to leave, she leaned over and kissed his cheek. "I'm sorry," she said, then let herself out of the car and ran for the house, the rain having picked up while they talked.

"I had an umbrella for you!" he called through his open window.

As she made her way up the steps to the porch, she saw Parker in the big chair by the fireplace, watching the entire exchange, and her cheeks burned in embarrassment.

Still, she couldn't stand outside all night, even if the porch did have an overhang to protect her from the rain, so she let herself inside.

Parker had risen from his seat and met her at the door. "Good date?"

She met his curious stare, still undecided about whether or not to tell him the truth about why she'd accepted the date in the first place. She would have mentioned it this afternoon, but his attitude, telling her what she could and couldn't do, had put her off.

"I've had better," she said honestly.

Her stomach chose that moment to growl in a loud, unladylike fashion.

Parker narrowed his gaze. "Didn't he feed you?"

"The steak was chewy," she admitted.

"And he didn't notice that you didn't eat?"

She merely shrugged.

"Come on." He grasped her hand in his larger one and pulled her toward the kitchen. "Your dad had leftover stew. I'll heat you up a bowl."

She couldn't turn down her favorite meal. "Thank you," she said, appreciating the gesture.

A little while later, he sat across from her at the table while she devoured her father's stew. "So tell me how you ended up here," she said, wanting to know more about this man she couldn't quite figure out.

"My family owns a company that supplies smart locks to corporations and defense contractors. Knight Time Technology. My older brother, Ethan, runs things, and my brother Sebastian, my sister, Sierra, and I all work there," he explained.

She placed her spoon down and looked at him. "A family business. That's nice. My sister moved away and I miss her."

"Having mine was a Godsend for me, to be honest."

She'd finished her dinner and pushed the bowl aside, leaning in to listen more closely. "How so?"

He hesitated, his expression more open and vulnerable than she'd seen since meeting him. "My mom died when I was thirteen. She had cancer."

Tears filled her eyes, the memory of losing her own mom under a year ago still fresh. "I'm so sorry," she whispered, feeling an unexpected bond with Parker, this man she'd been trying so hard not to like.

"Thanks. I know you understand."

But she couldn't imagine her beloved parent dying when she'd still been young and needed her in myriad ways.

He ran a hand through his hair, the subject obviously upsetting. "After that, my dad basically checked out. It was like he was no longer a parent. Ethan stepped up but he was only two years older than me, so it was tough on him. Still, he became our father figure, Sierra, Sebastian, and me. Made sure we did our homework, got to school, and kicked Sebastian's ass when he stepped out of line, which was often."

His sexy lips kicked up, obviously at the memory of his brother's antics. "Dad was there to buy him out of trouble but not to be there for him ... or any of us in the ways that mattered. He had a revolving door of wives and the four of us came to rely on each other. A lot."

"That's sad," she murmured.

"You have a great father. I only wish I had that kind of role model, but I have my brothers and sister."

His voice warmed as he spoke of them and it was obvious he loved his siblings, she thought, seeing a

67

softer side to Parker Knight. It made her nervous, liking him, lowering her guard in any way.

"Shit," he said with a shake of his head. "You asked me how I ended up here and I dove into my past. Point is, I came out here to check out one of the bigger lodges as a place where we can hold a corporate retreat. It didn't pan out and I decided to take my time heading back to Denver. I was driving through town when my car started acting up. And here I am."

"And you seem in no rush to get back."

"No, I'm not." He leaned forward in his seat, studying her for so long and so intently a flush rose to her face. Reaching out, he stroked a hand over her warm cheeks. "There's a lot to like here," he murmured.

At his touch, her body responded, nipples tightening, desire throbbing between her thighs. She was in so much freaking trouble, she thought, jumping up and taking the bowl to the sink.

His low chuckle reverberated through her.

"I need to get to sleep," she said. "I have to be up early to bake and take everything to Harper's." She was avoiding him and anything serious and she had no doubt he knew it, too.

"I'll help you with your baked goods and drive you in to get your car," he said, telling her what they would do. Not asking.

But when Parker gave orders, it didn't feel like he

was manipulating her, merely going out of his way to help her when she needed it.

And how could she be upset with him for that?

Chapter Four

EMILY AND PARKER sat at a table in the corner of a packed Harper's, the usual morning rush of people grabbing coffee and muffins great to see. She'd hired another barista to help serve, which eased the load and, as things finally slowed down, let Harper join Emily and Parker at a table, where they'd waited. Emily wanted to spend time with her friend before picking up her car, and Parker seemed in no rush to get back to the inn, hanging out with her for the morning.

She didn't know what to make of him tagging along with her or even remaining in Colorado when he had a life waiting for him in New York City.

She and Harper were discussing expanding again, Harper pushing for it, Emily hedging because she just didn't think she could get a loan from the bank. All the while, Parker listened intently.

She also worried about what would become of the town if her father sold, but she had to worry about her dad first and foremost and she didn't mention that thought out loud. Her priority was getting her dad to Florida. He'd had pneumonia this year and she wanted him where it was warm and he could be healthy.

"So how'd it go last night?" Harper asked when they were finished talking about expanding and going into business together, or rather, according to Harper, had put the discussion on hold.

Emily shot her friend a warning glance. She hadn't told Parker why she'd gone out with Matt because, for now, letting him think she'd wanted the date served her purpose, helping to keep him at a safe emotional distance.

"It sucked," Parker said, answering for her. "The asshole didn't realize she didn't eat and she was starving when she got home." He folded his arms across his broad chest. "Don't worry. I fed her."

Emily bit down on the inside of her cheek, hard, before coming to Matt's defense in front of Harper. "Matt's not an asshole!"

"He's not," Harper added. "He must have had a lot on his mind." But her friend's expression turned gleeful as she said,

"I guess it's a good thing she only went out with him to let him down gently then." She leaned in on her elbows. "You know, because she didn't want to humiliate him in front of you when he asked her out."

Emily shut her eyes and groaned, shaking her head

at her friend's obvious meddling in her life.

"Really," Parker said, eyeing Emily in a way that promised retribution. "You mean she went on a date and let me go crazy with jealousy ... on purpose?"

Had he actually admitted to being jealous? Shock settled inside her but Harper's next words brought her back to what she needed to focus on.

"That's our girl," Harper said without a hint of remorse for betraying Emily. Her best friend. Or former best friend, because Emily was going to disown her after this, for sure.

"I'm right here," she felt compelled to remind them both as they spoke about her as if she were invisible.

"Oh, I know. Believe me," Parker said. He looked delicious, wearing a pair of dark jeans, work boots, and a white knitted sweater. His blue eyes pinned her in place and she knew she was in trouble when they were alone.

Not the kind of trouble she'd have been in with Rex, with a barrage of humiliating words aimed to hit her where they hurt and belittled her ... no, something told her she was going to like Parker's form of punishment.

She squirmed in her chair, her body alive with possibilities, as he merely stared, his sexy mouth turning up in a grin.

"Excuse me." A man about Parker's age walked over to the table. "I'm sorry to bother you but you look familiar. Are you Parker Knight?"

Parker nodded, rising to his feet, his face coming alive with recognition. "Caleb Benson!" He walked over to the other man and gave him a man-type hug followed by a slap on the back. "How the hell are you?"

"Great. Married with two kids and I run a ski shop nearby."

"Yeah? How's business?" Parker asked.

"Great. We're right off the highway and we get a lot of traffic. I love it. It's everything I wanted and I'd even expand if I could, but I can barely keep up with the business I do have."

Parker nodded. "I'm thrilled for you." Knowing what it was like to be doing something he didn't love, he liked seeing a man find success and happiness at the same time.

"You should stop in."

"I will."

Emily rose from her seat just as Parker had turned her way. "Emily Stevens and Harper Sanders, this is—"

"Caleb Benson." Emily smiled. "Small town," she reminded Parker. "But how do you two know each other?"

Caleb's brown eyes opened wide. "Parker here was

the Alpine Ski World Cup Men's Champion back in
our prime days. If you didn't know about his mad
skills, how do *you* know Parker?"

Emily glanced at Parker in shock. The man was full
of surprises. "Parker came by the inn the other day
when his car broke down. I don't know him that well."

He stepped closer, until their bodies touched and
she was reminded that he wanted something to exist
between them.

"She knows enough," Parker said on a growl, then
glanced at Caleb. "I don't normally talk about those
days." His voice dropped as did his gaze. Something
about that time caused him a world of hurt.

Emily knew about hurt and loss. She knew about
pushing the pain so far down and deep she didn't have
to think about it on a daily basis. Except it was always
there, on the edges, threatening to come back and
make her cry at the oddest possible times. And Parker
had that same look in his eyes now that she saw in the
mirror at her most vulnerable points.

"I'm sorry, man. I forgot," Caleb said, wincing. He
obviously knew and felt bad. "That was insensitive of
me. Anyway, it was good to see you. And the offer to
stop by still stands."

Parker's expression relaxed and he smiled. "I'll be
there. It'll be good to catch up."

Caleb nodded, smiled at Harper, then Emily, and

walked away.

"Well, that was interesting," Harper said, as Parker held out Emily's chair for her to sit back down before joining her.

Emily frowned. "I'm sure it was good to see an old friend," she said to Parker, not wanting to force him to focus on whatever Caleb had touched on that was so sensitive for him.

"It was. Caleb and I skied together. He never medaled but he was good."

"Unlike you, Mr. Champion," Emily said, impressed with what she'd learned about him. "So you aren't just a corporate mogul but you're a ski champ. What other secrets are you hiding?" she teased him.

"None you want to know about. Now are you ready to get your car?" He pushed back his chair, a sure sign he was finished with the conversation.

She'd obviously treaded too close to his private pain. She hadn't meant to. "I am."

"And I need to get back to work. Text ya later," Harper said to Emily. "Bye, Parker. Be good." She winked at him and headed back around the counter.

Emily turned to Parker, who looked bothered, like he suddenly had more on his mind than he'd had since arriving at the inn. "Listen, you can head home. I'll just get my car and meet you there."

"I'll go with you. Make sure Matt heard you loud

and clear last night." Parker placed a hand on her back and she shivered at his warm touch, which she felt through the light sweater she wore.

She didn't need him making a point with Matt, but by the look on his face, she knew better than to make a scene. He wanted to join her? Let him.

One thing she'd learned this morning, there was a lot she didn't know about Parker Knight.

The question was, did she want to learn when doing so involved them getting closer?

AFTER AN UNCOMFORTABLE trip to the garage, where Parker hovered and Matt definitely realized he was the odd man out, Emily drove her car home. Parker disappeared with her dad, who wanted to give him a tour of the property, and she spent the day relaxing by the fire with a good book.

Later on, she headed to the kitchen to make dinner, a plain roasted chicken with vegetables and red potatoes. Then she decided a pie was in order and found herself peeling apples for a good part of her afternoon. Parker seemed to be busy, maybe with work, because he was on the phone when he returned with her dad, joined them for dinner, where he raved over her food, and then disappeared into his room again, saying he had calls to make.

The next couple of days were business as usual. Emily woke up early, baked, and Parker showed up to help her load the car and take her goods to Harper's. Sometimes they stayed and shared a cup of coffee, sometimes they went back to the inn, where she prepped for the next day.

Both he and her dad seemed busy, but where Parker was concerned, she minded her own business. He was here taking a break from his reality and he deserved not to be bothered by the people surrounding him. Even if she was insanely curious as to who he was talking to and what he was doing. In fact, the more he kept to himself, leaving her alone and not backing her against cars to kiss her, the crazier she became.

What happened to the man who'd told her he was jealous of her date with Matt? Who'd sat next to her at Harper's and gotten close enough to drive her insane with his hot body and masculine scent? Who'd said there was a lot to like here?

She glanced down at the bowl she'd been mixing … and had gotten lost in thought and forgotten to continue. "Dammit!"

Why did she care if the man was all but ignoring her? She didn't want him in her life, right? He was a city guy who liked to control things around him and she was finished with men like that. He'd be leaving eventually and she didn't need to get attached and end up with a broken heart.

So really, it was all for the best.

Wasn't it?

ONCE HE HAD a purpose, Parker immersed himself in the job he wanted to do at the inn. After taking a tour with James, making notes in his phone on what needed updating, renovating, and outright replacing, they spoke about who James wanted to hire. If he chose to give the job to locals, Parker was happy to do so. He wasn't interested in taking over, just paving the way for the man to have the inn of his and his wife's dreams. And he hoped Emily didn't bust his balls in the process.

He noticed that James hadn't gone out of his way to fill her in on his plans, so Parker didn't offer up the information that he was funding the renovation himself. That was between father and daughter, a place he did not belong. He wasn't comfortable withholding the news but it wasn't his to provide.

As for Emily, Parker had given a lot of thought to his conversation with James about her past relationship. She was obviously recovering from a serious situation that had hurt her a great deal. Parker himself seemed to trigger her, and coming on like a caveman wasn't going to help matters. As a result, he'd started to give her space to figure out if she wanted to get involved with him while he was here. In the meantime, he felt useful for the first time in a long time.

But as the days passed, he found it harder to keep his distance from Emily. Waking up and walking downstairs to the smell of her delicious treats baking in the kitchen, finding her hustling around the room, hair in a high bun or ponytail, adorable strands hanging around her face, sometimes humming, sometimes dancing to music in her earbuds as she worked, left him with a constant hard-on.

He stood in the doorway, watching her swivel her hips to whatever beat she heard in her ears, when his cell phone rang, startling her and causing her to drop the spoon she'd been holding. She glanced over and shot him an annoyed glare, then bent to pick up the utensil, giving him a perfect view of her ass as he answered the phone without looking at who was calling.

"Yeah?" He was annoyed at the interruption.

"Parker?"

"Sebastian. What's up?" He hadn't spoken to his younger brother since he'd gotten to Colorado. "Everything okay? Ashley good?"

"All fine. No worries. Ethan's just giving the rest of us hell because you've finally taken a vacation. What gives?"

His gaze on Emily, who was pouring batter into muffin tins, Parker couldn't help the grin that lifted his lips. "Let's just say I found something better than family business to occupy my time."

With the earbuds in, she didn't so much as flick a glance his way to indicate she'd heard him.

"Hah. Switzerland finally made a decision."

Parker rolled his eyes at that damned nickname his family had thrust upon him, first because of his time on the slopes and later because he was the most laid-back of the siblings, letting them make decisions around him and staying neutral unless he had something earth-shattering to say.

"So you finally found a woman who does it for you. Let me be the first to congratulate you," Sebastian said. "I was beginning to think celibacy was going to be your permanent state."

Parker rolled his eyes. "Shut the fuck up," he muttered to his brother.

Sebastian laughed. "Come on. Someone has to give you shit and Ethan's too busy being an ass."

Parker shook his head. "What are we going to do about him?" he asked, concerned about his oldest sibling.

"We'll intervene when you get home. When will that be?"

Not any time soon, Parker thought. "Couldn't tell you. But I'll be in touch," he promised Sebastian, as Emily slid her muffins into the oven and closed the door.

"Okay, take care. Don't do anything I wouldn't do, which leaves the field pretty wide open with whoever this woman is." Sebastian disconnected the call and Parker slid the phone into his jeans pocket.

Emily's back was to him and Parker decided he'd had enough distance. He'd intended to give her a chance to come to him but she wasn't that type of woman. He'd just have to offer her an out should she want one.

Walking up behind her, he slid his hands over her waist and pressed a kiss to her neck, inhaling the sweet scent that was Emily when he wasn't smelling chocolate or the baked goodness that surrounded her.

"Yum," he whispered in her ear at the same time he pulled her against him.

"Parker!" She jumped in surprise, but instead of jerking away, she leaned back into him, her ass pressing against his groin.

He swallowed a groan, willing to put up with the discomfort in order to be near her. "I don't want to keep my hands off you," he whispered against her ear.

"Then don't." She turned in his arms, facing him. "You've been avoiding me." Hurt flickered in her pretty brown eyes, an emotion he'd never intended to put there.

He slid a finger over her cheek, stroking the smooth skin. "I thought you needed time away from me."

Her lips pursed in a pout he wanted to kiss away. "What I don't need is you making decisions for me." She locked her fingers around his neck, meeting his gaze. "Everything about you makes me nervous but maybe that's a good thing. I need to face my fears, right?" she said, more to herself than to him.

"You're afraid of me?" That didn't sound like a good thing.

She shook her head. "I'm afraid of what you re-mind me of." She paused. "*Who* you remind me of. But that's not fair. So for the time that you're here, I'm going to try to be more open-minded."

He nodded in approval. "I appreciate that. I never want to be someone who frightens you."

"You don't." She spread her fingers through his hair and his body sensitized at her touch.

He inhaled long and hard, the scent of cinnamon reaching his nose. "What are you baking?" he asked.

"Oh, I see. You just want me for my goodies," she said with a grin.

He chuckled, low and deep. "That I do," he said, just not elaborating on which of her goodies he desired most.

"I'm making cinnamon rolls."

He nuzzled her neck, enjoying being this close to her. "Let me take you out."

"Like on a real date?" She sounded excited at the prospect.

"Yeah. Like on a real date. What's your favorite restaurant nearby?"

She tipped her head back and met his gaze. "Hmm. There's a steak place in the center of town. Gabriel's. It's our nicest restaurant. Which isn't saying much. Nice jeans are perfect. I don't need anything more than that." She eyed him warily, as if expecting him to disagree.

He patted the tip of her nose with his finger. "Just because I'm from Manhattan doesn't mean I need an upscale restaurant to make me happy. It's more about the company than the place. And you're all I need to enjoy the night."

A smile lit up her face. "Then I'd love to go out with you."

More than pleased with her response, he leaned in and sealed his lips over hers, moaning at the sweetness he tasted there. She tangled her hands back into his hair and kissed him as he backed her against the counter, his dick settled into the cradle of her hips, pressing hard into her.

"Your father," he muttered, trying to be aware that he wasn't in the right place to make out with the man's daughter.

"He's out for breakfast with a friend. He won't be home for hours." She tugged on his hair, urging him to stop talking and resume kissing.

He did as she silently requested, recapturing her mouth and thrusting inside. What happened next was an immediate dueling of tongues and grinding of hips, the desire that they'd been holding in check boiling over. He rocked against her, taking his cues from the soft sighs and moans coming from deep in her throat.

He eased one hand between them, lifted her apron, and unbuttoned her jeans, sliding his fingers beneath her panties, coming into contact with bare skin.

He swore at the heat and slickness that greeted him, his cock throbbing against the harsh denim of his pants. Gritting his teeth, he focused on her, his fingers gliding over her smooth skin before settling on her clit.

Her hips bucked and she groaned, pulling tighter on his hair. "Easy, sweetheart. I've got you."

As he began to circle his finger over the tight bud, her dampness eased his way as he worked to bring her higher. She shuddered against him, her hips circling in rhythm with his increasingly harder caress.

He wanted to see her come for him. Wanted her to

come hard. So when she got too deep into her head and fears, she'd remember this. Him.

He licked at her lips, continued kissing her while he pinched her clit and she screamed, a sound he caught in his mouth, as she shook and trembled against him.

He lifted his head in time to see the rosy glow in her cheeks and the dazed look in her eyes as she came back to reality. Damned if a part of him wasn't proud of that look and fucking aroused by it.

He kissed her nose, slid his hand out from her pants, and helped her pull herself together, buttoning her jeans and straightening her apron.

Grinning, she smoothed his hair with her fingers. "I made a mess."

She could pull his hair any time, he thought. "You good?"

She nodded. "I need to clean up. The kitchen. I mean I need to clean up the kitchen," she said, her blush a sweet and refreshing difference from the more experienced women who propositioned him back home.

"Well, I'll leave you to it. Oh, and Emily?"

"Yes?" She brushed a stray strand of hair off her face.

"Thank you. I'll keep the memory of you with me all day." He lifted his hand and slid his fingers into his mouth, licking first one, then the other, taking in the flavor that was all Emily's. "And block off tomorrow night for me. I'll be making reservations at Gabriel's."

Her eyes wide at his actions, she nodded. "And I'll be looking forward to it." Her voice was husky.

She was shaken. Just how he wanted her. Off-kilter. For him.

✧   ✧   ✧

EMILY'S BODY TINGLED all day and well into the night. Her dreams included Parker and his talented hands skimming over her body in myriad ways. He hadn't shaved since he'd arrived at the inn and his scruff was even sexier than his clean-shaven look and kissing him was delicious. She woke up in the middle of the night in a heated sweat, knowing he was in the room across the hall, then found it impossible to fall back to sleep.

So when noise woke her up in the morning, the one morning she didn't have to bake, she was exhausted and in a pissy mood.

She pulled on a pair of sweats and a hoodie and walked out of her room, heading downstairs, where she found her father talking to a man wearing a hard hat. The noise above her continued.

"What's going on?" she asked, confused.

Her father glanced at her, looking sheepish. He

turned to the man, who she now recognized as William Cartwright, a contractor. "Can we talk more later?"

"Sure thing." He nodded and headed out the door, closing it behind him.

"Dad? What's going on? It sounds like they're working on the roof." She pointed to the ceiling above them.

Her father nodded. "We need a new one. You know that. We leak in every rain or snowstorm."

She bit the inside of her cheek. "But we don't have the money."

"About that…" He gestured for her to come over to the sofa in the center of the family room and take a seat.

She settled in warily and he eased down beside her. "I got the money to fund a full renovation."

She blinked. "What? How?"

"Parker offered the money. I didn't want to take it but he insisted. He said I could pay him back with interest and I gave him free room and board. It's the least I could do."

Parker. The man she'd decided she could trust. The man who'd given her an intense orgasm with his fingers alone. That Parker.

She felt as if she'd been punched in the stomach. "What the hell?" She'd told him she was worried about her father. That he belonged in Florida with her sister, where he'd be more relaxed and healthier.

Yet here he was, thinking he knew what was best, throwing money at a situation he knew nothing about.

The more she thought about it, the angrier she became.

"Em." Her father called out her name, bringing her out of her thoughts. "It was your mother's dream and mine. I want this."

Her dad had been a good accountant, solid with numbers. Not so much with reality. He held on to dreams sometimes like a little boy, without thinking through the details and full ramifications.

"Who's going to run it?" she asked. "I can't prep and bake at the same time. There's cleaning, laundry, meals, snack food, being there for the guests…"

He ran a hand through his hair, messing it up so it stood in spikes. "One thing at a time, okay? I want to see it through."

"So you can get more money for the property when you sell?" she asked hopefully.

"I'm not ready to discuss that right now." He rose to his feet. "I have a lot of plans to fix this place up and that's where my focus is at the moment."

She suddenly felt like her life was spiraling out of control. She jumped up to her feet.

"Em?"

"I'm going to put on my sneakers and go for a walk," she said, needing fresh air.

"Honey, it's going to be great. I promise you. You just need to relax."

She shook her head. Relax. Right. From owing Parker money to her father's sudden desire to run the inn … she didn't know what to think or feel.

But she did know she was angry at Parker for butting into her family, where he had no business getting involved. She strode to the side entrance, where she kept her shoes, and pulled on a pair of sneakers along with her jacket and headed out the door just as Parker pulled in, driving her dad's car.

She met him as he exited the vehicle.

"Hey, beautiful."

She clenched her jaw, determined that his charm wasn't going to work on her right now. "What's going on with your rental, by the way?" she asked him instead of saying hello.

He narrowed his gaze, a flush rising to his face. "I told the rental company to come deal with it on their time."

"Because you're staying here for a while."

He shoved his hands into his jacket pockets. "Yes … you knew that."

"But I didn't know you were giving my father money to fix this place!" She raised her hand toward the top of the inn, where men were working and banging as they put on an entirely new roof. And that was just the beginning of Lord knew what her father had in mind. Or Parker, for that matter. She had no idea how involved he was in this whole venture.

He groaned. "I didn't think it was my place to tell you. It was your father's."

"Then how about it wasn't your place to offer him the money to begin with?"

"Why not?" He leaned against the car as he studied her. "Because what you want for your father isn't what he wants for himself?"

Put that way, she didn't like how it sounded. "I just want what's best for him. Did he tell you he had a bad case of pneumonia this year that put him in the hospital?"

"No."

"Did he discuss his plans for how he would run the place once you fund it? Who would cook, clean, take care of the guests alongside him?"

"Well … no. But I assumed he had a plan that was in place when he bought the inn with your mom. And he seems pretty damned healthy to me. People get sick but they don't always die."

She narrowed her gaze. "You suck." Hurt and angry, knowing he'd hit on her greatest fear for her father, she spun and started to walk down the road, needing to be alone.

"Emily!"

He called her name but she didn't turn around.

"Emily, wait." He rushed after her, catching up to her easily.

She headed down a path she'd discovered when she needed a break from taking care of her mom and walked on. Parker kept pace beside her, not talking but not letting her be alone, either.

Suddenly and without warning, with memories of her mom's illness and fear of losing her father overwhelming her, she started to cry.

Chapter Five

PARKER WALKED BESIDE Emily, her anger obvious with each step she took. As much as he'd anticipated upsetting her, he felt bad anyway. Family was a touchy subject. He understood that more than most. Still, he was taken off guard when he heard the first sniffle beside him, then glanced over and realized she'd started crying.

"Hey." He grasped her elbow and pulled her to a stop. "I'm sorry. I didn't mean to hurt you."

"It's not that. Well, not directly." She brushed at her damp cheeks. "It's more about my mother. And worrying about my father. It all comes back to overwhelm me at the oddest times. And it forces me to act in a way I think is protecting him." She pulled in a deep breath. "I don't expect you to understand."

"Actually, I do. It's cold. Let's go inside and talk."

She wrinkled her nose. "It's noisy inside. Let's go to Harper's. I'll text her, she'll save us a table, we can get some hot chocolate and talk."

He liked the fact that she wasn't holding a grudge.

She wasn't happy with him but she was open to talking.

A little while later, they were at a private table in the corner of the coffee shop, the usually nosey Harper keeping to herself behind the counter.

Two hot chocolates sat in front of them loaded with whipped cream, and from the way Emily's eyes opened wide, Harper knew her friend well.

She dipped her finger into the whipped cream and sucked the tip into her mouth, causing Parker to groan.

Her gaze flew to his and a blush stained her cheeks. "Oops."

He laughed but sobered, not wanting to let the serious moment of earlier go. Not when he thought she needed to talk about her mom and her grief … and the unfair expectations she was placing on her father as a result.

He placed a hand on hers, causing her gaze to come to his. "About your mom … have you ever had a good cry? Or did you hold it in to protect your father?" he asked quietly.

She swallowed hard. "I cried. We're on opposite sides of the house, Dad and I, so it was okay. And I had Harper to listen to me when I needed to talk or vent. And Dad likes talking about Mom and good memories."

He nodded. "That's good." Unlike his brother, who didn't want his dead wife's name even mentioned ... but then again, Mandy had betrayed him. It wasn't even in the same ballpark as what had happened to James and Emily.

"Look, I know you lost your mom when you were younger," she said. "It wasn't fair of me to say that you wouldn't understand." She blinked, her lashes damp with unshed tears, and his stomach clenched at the sight.

"But I didn't have a parent left that I loved the way you do your father. That's different. But I have experienced loss." And he wanted her to know about it.

Like his brother Ethan, Parker never spoke about that time in his life, not even with his siblings, but for some reason, he wanted to share with Emily so she'd know him. He wanted her to see him as more than some charming guy who'd swooped into her life, thrown cash at her father, and thought he knew best.

It was his turn to swallow hard. "I was engaged."

Her eyes opened wide but she remained silent, letting him tell the story in his own time. "Rina and I were close in school, we both loved skiing, and she understood my love of competing, medaling, and turning pro. The relationship took a natural progression. But to make a long story short, we were driving one night and a car came out of nowhere, broadsiding us. I was just coming back from an injury on the slopes and the impact shattered my knee … but Rina, she died instantly."

"Oh my God. I'm so sorry," Emily said, wrapping her arms around him and cushioning him in warmth, understanding, and everything that was Emily.

The lump in his throat from talking about that time was painful. He swallowed it down and pulled away, glancing at her. "I just don't want you to think that I don't understand emotions or pain. Or that I intended to barge into your life and take over like whoever hurt you before did."

She opened her mouth but he shook his head. "Not now. We don't need to get into that today." Someday soon, he wanted to know all about her. But she was suffering now and she needed to cope with her current issues with the inn and her father. "Look. You can't protect your father from life."

"But I can make it easier for him to live out his years and be healthy. Relaxed. Happy. In Florida, where it's warmer."

"What if the inn makes him happy?" Parker asked, because he'd seen the gleam in the older man's eyes when he spoke of renovations and had accepted Parker's offer.

"Or what if he just thinks it does because it was

my mother's dream?"

He groaned, realizing he wasn't going to sway her on this subject. "Okay, just don't fight with him over it. It's not what you need in your relationship and working on the inn makes him happy."

Emily opened and closed her mouth before deciding on what to say. "As long as he sells it at the end," she finally muttered under her breath.

With a nod, Parker tucked those words away to think about later.

"Would you understand if I rescheduled dinner?" she asked. "I'm not in the mood to go out in public and make small talk with people I know that I'm bound to run into."

"Sure." He understood. He glanced at their probably cooled hot chocolate. "Now let's drink."

She shot him a grateful smile and picked up her cup, taking a long sip, letting what remained of the whipped cream create a foamy white mustache.

Unable to resist, he leaned in for a kiss, then swiped his tongue over her upper lip and groaned. "You taste so fucking good."

"I think that's the whipped cream."

"I beg to differ. It's all you." He grabbed her neck and pulled her into him, sliding his tongue over her mouth once more before dipping inside.

She gripped his shoulders and the kiss got hotter,

deeper, only an awareness of his surroundings keeping him from hauling her into his lap and making her his in the most carnal sense.

She licked his lips back despite the fact that he hadn't tasted the hot chocolate yet, and the feel of her had him shifting uncomfortably in his seat, his cock hard and ready. It was going to be damned difficult to convince himself he wasn't taking her here.

Until the distinctive sound of a male throat clearing interrupted them, and when he reluctantly broke off the kiss and glared at the intruder, he found himself looking at a man in a three-piece suit.

"So this is why you left me? So you could degrade yourself by practically having sex in public? I had no idea you were into voyeurism," the man said, his voice dripping with disdain.

Before Parker could react, he felt rather than saw Emily shrink back from him and knew immediately who he was dealing with. No, he didn't have a name or the full story, but the only one who could make his girl react like this was the asshole who had done a number on her.

And she *was* his girl and Parker intended to make that clear, starting now.

He rose to his feet. "Can I help you? Because from where I'm standing, you're interrupting a private moment."

The man looked like a typical stuffed shirt... As much as Parker hated to admit it, he reminded him of Ethan before Mandy's betrayal had sent him spiraling. Like Parker looked when he went to the office back in Manhattan. Emily had called him city boy, and looking at this man, he now knew why the notion put her on edge.

"Parker Knight," he said, not extending his hand for a shake.

"Rex Mason and that's my *wife* whose mouth you had your tongue in," the other man said, disgusted.

Parker blinked at the word *wife*.

In her chair, Emily let out a sound, then seeming to gather her courage, she rose to her feet. "That's soon-to-be ex-wife, Rex. We're legally separated."

The man scowled. "Not by my choice and you know it."

"If it were up to me, our marriage would be over already. The state of Illinois wants us separated for two years ... unless you're finished contesting my petition?" she asked, sounding hopeful.

"Don't be ridiculous. You belong with me." Apparently Emily's ex was pompous as well as dense.

Harper had joined them in a show of support for her friend. "This is my shop and I don't want you here, Rex."

"Oh, great. The peanut gallery speaks. I don't need

you filling Emily's ears with bullshit about me. I'm here to see my wife and you can't stop me." He took a step forward and Parker stopped him with a hand to his chest.

Emily folded her arms over her chest. "I don't want to see you."

"But I flew in and drove all this way to be with you. I thought I could stay at the inn and we could talk out our differences."

"No." Parker spoke before Emily could. "She already said she doesn't want to see you."

"*She* can speak for herself," Emily said and Parker realized he'd made a mistake.

He couldn't do anything that would remind her of her controlling husband. The fact that they were still married irritated him, but the law was the law. They were legally *separated* and she wanted nothing to do with the man. Parker didn't let himself wonder why he cared so much or what he could actually do with her, considering his life was in New York. He just knew he was feeling particularly possessive about this woman and he refused to let anyone push her around. She was his while he was here.

"You are not staying at my family's inn," Emily said. Having found her voice, she stood up for herself against Rex.

"Because of the construction? I was there earlier

and saw the work being done. Is that what's keeping you here in this small town? You're an innkeeper now? Surely you want more for yourself. I can live with the construction if it means we can spend time together."

She shook her head. "No. I don't want you there regardless of the construction and that's my family's business you're disparaging, so watch it."

He narrowed his gaze, obviously not used to her talking back to him, but Emily went on.

"And since it's the only place to sleep in the area, you're going to have to drive back and stay somewhere else in another town. You wasted a trip coming here."

His frown marred his otherwise perfect appearance, the well-cut blond hair, expensive suit, and tie. "Think about the life we had together, the penthouse and all your gorgeous clothes. They're still in the closet, just waiting for you."

He looked her over then, his gaze traveling from the top of her messy bun to the sneakers she wore on her feet.

A look Parker found downright adorable, appealing, and infinitely sexy.

Her soon-to-be ex's scowl deepened as he took in Emily's appearance. "Surely you can see you've let yourself go. You haven't lost the weight you put on when... Well, never mind that."

Emily winced, her hand coming to brace her stomach.

Parker narrowed his gaze.

"And shouldn't you have gotten this muffin baking and waiting on other people out of your system by now?" Rex asked, obviously frustrated. Oblivious to everything, he continued to speak, putting his foot in his mouth with every sentence.

Lord only knew what Emily had once seen in this guy.

"Come home and things can be like they used to," Rex cajoled in a sickening voice.

Jesus Christ. Was this guy for real, insulting her like that and then asking her to come home? "Hey now–" Parker stepped forward but Emily spoke up.

"It's like you never knew me at all," she said.

"I know the woman you became. The one you were always meant to be."

The one he clearly had tried to mold her into, Parker realized. He'd had enough of this upright, ridiculous ass looking to change the perfect woman standing in front of him. "Time to go," he said. "And if you say no, I have no problem escorting you out."

Before he could grab the man's arm, Rex got the hint. "I'm leaving. But this isn't finished. *We* aren't finished." He adjusted his suit jacket and strode out of the shop.

Emily blew out a huge breath, her shoulders dropping in relief as the bells rang above the door, signaling he was gone.

"Oh, honey! I hate that asshole." Harper pulled Emily into a huge hug and quickly released her.

"Thanks for having my back," she said to her friend.

"Any time and you know it. I have to get back to work." Harper rushed back behind the counter and Emily turned her gaze on Parker.

"Don't say it," Parker said before she could turn her wrath on him. "I shouldn't have made any proclamations or decisions about whether or not he could stay. That was *your* choice to make."

A more relaxed smile edged her lips. "Who said you weren't teachable?" she asked and he was happy to see the visit hadn't left her on edge and irritable. She blew out a long breath. "I appreciate you saying that."

He nodded. "So…" He met her gaze, then had to state what was on his mind. "You're married?"

✧　✧　✧

HEARING PARKER SAY the word *married*, Emily winced. "Legally separated. And though I probably should have mentioned it to you, I honestly try not to think about Rex or anything having to do with my life or time with him. I'm just counting down the days

103

until the divorce becomes final."

"He doesn't want to let go," Parker said.

"He's like a dog with a bone. He got his teeth into me and has claimed me as his own. What I don't understand is why?"

A soft expression took over his features. "Because you're everything a man could want," he told her and her body went warm all over.

"Except I'm not what *he* wants, something he never failed to remind me of. You heard him. He wanted to change me from the day we met… Still does. And I let him."

She looked away, embarrassed by how weak she'd been when it came to Rex. But she'd been a small-town girl alone in the big city, thinking that's what she wanted. Then she met an exciting man who swept her off her feet and she hadn't realized she was turning into his vision of her until the deed was done.

"I'd expect him to take one look at me now and think he was lucky to be done with me." She gestured to her appearance, hair in a messy updo, sweats, very little makeup. And yeah, the extra weight she'd put on when she'd been pregnant with his baby, something she did not want to get into with Parker. At least not now. "He wants me back the way things were."

"And that's not happening." Parker pulled her into his arms and she hated to admit she felt safe there.

Once she'd seen Parker side-by-side with Rex, the differences had been stark. Her city boy was a sexy guy with nice clothes, an amazing personality, and a tendency to exert his will on occasion. But he never failed to look at her as if she were the most beautiful woman on the planet, no matter what she wore, and he never once belittled her. Rex had made sure to get in his digs, even today during his pitiful attempt to get her back into his world. A place she wasn't going. No matter what.

When they arrived back at the inn, her father was waiting in the main room, pacing and looking unhappy.

"Dad?" She stepped toward him, not holding a grudge or wanting to fight with him over the inn. "I'm sorry I lost my temper," she said.

He held out his arms and pulled her into a hug, kissing the top of her head. "I know. It's all good. We'll work it out," he promised her. Only once she'd stepped away did he sigh and say, "Rex was here earlier."

Behind her, a silent Parker stiffened at the mere mention of the man's name.

She nodded. "He found me in town."

"I didn't tell him where you were. Not that I knew. But I assumed you went to Harper's. Did he bother you? Because he tried to get me to let him stay here and I told him absolutely not." Her father rubbed his hands together nervously.

"It's fine, Dad. I'm fine."

"We handled him," Parker said, coming up behind her and wrapping an arm around her waist.

She didn't know what to make of his possessiveness. He was staying for a while but they both knew it was temporary. But after her revelation today about the differences between him and Rex, and his obvious dedication to her family, she was going to indulge for the time he was here, and she leaned back into him.

Her father seemed to relax at their words and the fact that they presented a united front.

She hoped he wasn't too disappointed when Parker left after he finished helping with the inn. It was going to be hard enough for her to get over him without adding her dad's feelings to the mix.

✧　✧　✧

BECAUSE OF HER lifestyle in Chicago, Emily had sexy lingerie that she'd purchased for Rex's pleasure, something she didn't like to think about anymore. When she'd left, she hadn't taken much with her, especially in the way of nighties, but she did have one with a tag that she'd never worn before.

Later that night, alone in her room, she dangled the short piece of silk and lace from her finger, staring at it as she considered the possibility of slipping on the garment and walking across the hall to Parker's room. Her nipples tightened at the thought and her sex pulsed with desire.

Obviously she wanted to be with him and she knew better than to think he'd turn her away. Their chemistry was off-the-charts hot. Which meant she didn't need to be nervous.

Still, her stomach fluttered as she gathered her courage and slipped into the negligee. A glance in the mirror, a fluff of her hair, and she then had to talk herself into believing he wouldn't mind the soft, rounded belly she still had. Thank you, Rex, for reminding her of that fact. Not that she ever forgot the reason behind the stomach but she'd managed to come to terms with the miscarriage and was even grateful that it meant she wasn't tied to Rex permanently in any way. But she'd still mourned the loss of her baby.

She smoothed the silk down her hips, drew a deep breath, and opened the door to her room – at the same time a bare-chested Parker stepped through his doorway wearing a pair of unbuttoned jeans, appearing extremely sexy with his mussed hair, bare feet, and the tapered vee of hair that trailed down his abdomen.

"I hope you're coming to see me," he said, his darkened blue gaze trailing over her negligee, his stare focused on her pointed nipples, traveling down her bare legs.

"And if I am? What would you do with me?" She stepped forward and found herself hauled into his arms.

He lifted her and she wrapped her legs around his waist, his mouth coming down hard on hers. They'd been dancing around this attraction since he'd arrived, her not wanting to admit one look at him had her addicted. There was no denying their desire now.

He walked them into his room and slammed the door behind him.

Next thing she knew, he'd placed her down on the bed. Standing over her, he stripped off his clothes until he was naked, his gorgeous body bared. His cock caught her attention, hard, thick, and very erect. A distinct pulse throbbed between her legs at the sight. A drop of pre-come pooled at the head and she moaned at the desire to taste him that overwhelmed her, surprising her with its intensity.

"As much as I appreciate the silk and lace, I need to feel your skin against mine," he muttered, gliding the nightie up and over her body, tossing it on the floor beside his clothes.

His gaze settled on the bare vee between her legs. "Fuck. You could have prepared me."

"Once I worked up the nerve to put on the lingerie, I figured what was the point of underwear?" She felt heat rise to her cheeks at the admission.

"I like the way you think." He kissed the tip of her nose, her lips, trailed his way over her chest, his erection gliding against her flesh as he made his way down her body. "That's what I mean. You feel fantastic," he said gruffly, his hips jerking his cock against her thigh.

He was big and it had been a long time for her. Over a year, really, and she knew this was going to be epic. But she couldn't focus on what would happen, because the sensations flooding her body called to her now.

His mouth paused in its travel at her breasts, licking his way across one until he reached her nipple. His lips latched on, suckling and tweaking, grazing the tight nub with his teeth, and she felt the erotic pull deep inside her sex. When he was obviously satisfied he'd tortured one sensitive nipple enough, he moved to the other side, giving it the same treatment.

She writhed beneath him, overly responsive and unused to the long span of attention he was giving her body. She knew what that said about her past relationship, but she didn't care about that, hadn't in a while, and shoved thoughts of it away now.

After having his fill, he lowered himself to her sex, took a long, what would have been embarrassing look,

109

had he not appeared so pleased with what he saw. His eyes darkened, a muscle ticked in his jaw, and a low groan escaped his throat. Then he took her with a lap of his tongue that had her body bowing off the bed.

He placed a hand over her belly, holding her in place, as he sucked, licked, and devoured her sex. She'd never been the focus of a man's attention this way, never had a guy so clearly enjoy her as Parker was doing.

The longer he spent pleasuring her, the higher her body soared, and she grappled, her fingers trying to grab the comforter to center her, but nothing was going to stop the pleasure rolling over her body. And she really didn't want it to as, without warning, she came, her body bucking against his talented mouth, lost in sensation. He kept up the delicious torment until she began to pull away, her body too sensitive.

She immediately reached down, wrapping her hand around his velvety hard erection, the desire to taste him returning now that she'd come back to earth herself. She started with a pump of her hand up and down his shaft until he gripped her wrist, stilling her movement.

"I want to come inside you," he said.

"But I want my turn to touch and taste you." She looked up at him, batting her eyelashes in an attempt to get her way.

He grinned, studying her with an intensity that unnerved her. "Fine but we do it my way."

She narrowed her gaze, suddenly wary and thinking she shouldn't have pushed the point.

"Come up here," he said, his voice a demand.

She wrinkled her nose in confusion.

"As in come put your knees on either side of my head. I do you. You do me," he said, his tone husky, his desire clear.

"Sixty-nine?" she squeaked, never having done anything so … adventurous or intimate before. At least it felt intimate, putting her body in that position.

"That's my deal. I make you come at the same time," Parker said, his voice almost daring her to take him up on his command.

She knew he was here for a short time. Knew she'd never have the chance to be with a man who turned her on the same way ever again. Parker was different. She *felt* differently about him and chemistry like this was rare. She'd never felt anything like it before.

Drawing a deep breath, she climbed up to where he waited, turned away from him, and positioned herself over his face, mortification consuming her. Until he licked her, a slow, luscious stroke of his tongue that had her entire body burning up.

"You taste like those sweet goodies you bake. Now lie down, baby, and let's get this going."

She stretched out over him and found his cock waiting for her. She treated him to the same lick he gave her, sliding her mouth slowly over his shaft.

He groaned, his hands coming up to grip her hips in a way that told her she'd have bruises afterwards. The thought aroused her even more. What happened next defied description and rational thought. Somehow she managed to suck him, up and down, hollowing out her lips and licking at the head. Wrapping her hand around the base of his erection, she slid her hand up and down in time to the movement of her mouth.

He groaned, thrusting his hips upward, and she swallowed over the head that grazed her throat and almost caused her to gag but she managed to hold off. He rewarded her by sucking, licking, and darting his tongue inside her, his mouth taking her places she'd never dreamed of.

She rocked against him, managing to keep him in her mouth and work him with her hand while he brought her higher and higher, her climax so close she could almost reach for it.

His tongue flicked at her clit and she shattered, grinding herself against his mouth, and seconds later, he was climaxing, too, coming down her throat as she struggled to swallow and keep up.

When she came to herself, he grasped her hips and

rolled her to her side. "C'mere," he said in a gruff voice.

She flipped and crawled up to him, letting him pull her into his arms, where he cushioned her in the most amazing embrace.

"I have to admit, I didn't envision *that* as our first time together," she said into his chest.

He kissed the top of her head. "Me, neither, but it was fucking incredible. Now let me catch my breath and then I want to know what it feels like to come inside that sweet pussy."

She pressed her lips to the hair on his chest, pushing herself up until her face was centimeters from his. Looking into his blue eyes, she fell a little, telling herself it was normal, that she wasn't usually a casual-sex kind of girl. So of course she had feelings for Parker. But she knew what this was ... and what it wasn't. What it was, was temporary and she was going to enjoy every moment while he was here.

He grasped the back of her neck in his hand and sealed his mouth over hers, gliding his tongue over her lips, and she was lost. He pushed her back until she lay against the mattress, his body coming over hers.

She gazed up at him as his cock nudged at the entrance of her sex.

He groaned. "Be right back," he said before she could remind him they needed protection. He strode into the bathroom, returning with a strip of condoms.

"You came prepared," she said. The thought was sobering. Of course, this man could have his pick of women anywhere he went.

"It's not what it looks like," he said, rejoining her on the bed. "I haven't traveled in years but they were in my Dopp Kit."

She believed him. He had no reason to lie and she was glad he had protection because she didn't and that would have derailed their night.

He looked to her for confirmation that she was okay, that they were fine, and her gaze fell to his still-hard erection.

"Well, what are you waiting for?" she asked in reply.

He ripped off one packet and tore into it, pulling out the condom and rolling it over his thick, straining shaft.

Watching him, she moaned, barely aware as the sound escaped from the back of her throat and her sex spasmed in anticipation of taking him inside her.

He grasped her hands and lifted them over her head. "Hold on," he said, hooking them onto the spindles on the headboard.

Eyes wide, she curled her hands around them and let him take charge.

"Now bend your knees."

She did as he said and he eased her legs back, exposing her to him as he aligned himself at her entrance and pushed himself inside. She groaned at the initial invasion that quickly turned to pleasure as he filled her, gliding out and sliding back in, her wetness lubricating his way until he bottomed out inside her, their bodies connecting completely.

"You feel so damn good." His warm breath fanned her ear as he trembled on top of her.

"So do you." She squeezed her inner muscles around him and they both groaned, the action prompting him to move.

His hands braced on either side of her head, he began to thrust into her, short, deliberate pumps of his hips followed by longer, more drawn-out glides that had her body in turmoil, the physical sensations more than she could take. But he didn't let up and she felt herself spiraling out of control.

There were defining moments in her life, things that she'd never forget, painful ones and out-of-this-world ones, and this moment with Parker fell into the latter. He was forever defining what sex should be.

He brought her to the peak, the waves of delicious sensation taking her higher and closer to climax. He reached between them and rubbed his thumb over her nipple, squeezing it between his fingers so hard she felt it in her core. Her hips arched, her body searching for more friction, more feeling. Just more.

Unable to keep her own hands off him any longer, she released her grip from the headboard and pulled at his hair as he slammed into her over and over again. She climaxed without warning, hard, fast, her entire body consumed by blinding heat and fire. And he followed her over, coming with a roar in her ear, his powerful body stilling as his release washed over him.

After he'd gotten up, disposed of the condom, and returned, he climbed back into bed, pulling her into him, his breathing rough and labored, matching her own.

"You're amazing." He wrapped himself around her, kissing her neck.

"You're pretty spectacular yourself." She swallowed over the lump in her throat, the one that told her emotions were involved despite the fact that she'd only known him a few days.

Short term, she reminded herself. "What did you decide to do about finding a place to hold your corporate retreat?"

"I put it on the back burner. But Ethan's called a few times. I just ignored him." He chuckled. "That's new for my brother. He'll live. But eventually I probably should look into alternatives."

She knew the area better than he did. "What if I know of a perfect resort I can show you? My dad

116

seems to have things under control here. You've funded him, you've approved his ideas, we can go for a few days and look around?"

She'd take whatever time alone with him she could get.

He rolled her onto her back, coming down on top of her. "Are you suggesting we go away for a few days?"

"Are you opposed to the idea?"

He nudged her sex with his hard-again cock. "Does it feel like I'm opposed?"

She grinned. "No, it feels like you're ready to go again."

"That's a yes. To a ski lodge … and hand me a condom," he said in a husky voice that had her body clenching in need.

Chapter Six

J AMES STEVENS WAS a romantic at heart, so when Emily told her dad she and Parker were headed out of town to scout locations for his corporate retreat, James was all for the idea. She wasn't worried about leaving him alone with Rex lurking around because her ex had a pattern. He came and he went, disappearing again while he regrouped for another attempt at bringing her back to Chicago.

What she did worry about was her father getting his hopes up that something more would come of her relationship with Parker other than friendship. He didn't need to know that *more* already had occurred, because Parker was leaving eventually.

But for now, they were going on a trip and she was excited. She packed her light parka because it was colder in the mountains even in April, boots, and her favorite cargo snow pants. In addition, she added the nightie he'd flung off her before she'd had a chance to wear it, lace bra, and panties, though she hoped not to wear them at all.

Carly Phillips

All set, she met Parker at the bottom of the stairs. She was still struck by his beard each time she saw him and had the scruff marks on her thighs to remember it by. She squirmed as she approached him, her sex tingling at the memory.

But she was unable to contain her excitement over their trip. "I'm ready!"

"I can see that. I'm impressed you've packed everything in one carry-on."

"Used to more high-maintenance women?" she asked, trying not to be jealous.

"Truth?"

"And nothing but," she said, bracing herself.

"There haven't been many women in my life and none in a long time," he said, taking her by surprise.

She stared at him. "But ... that really shocks me," she admitted. "Is it because of your fiancée who died?" This time she tried not to be jealous of a dead woman who was long gone and whose memory nobody could compete against.

"Again, no. We've got a long trip and a lot of time to talk." Reaching out, he grabbed her hand. "And we will."

She looked into his beautiful blue eyes and saw pain. Pain he normally hid well, but she already knew about his fiancée's death and a ski career he no longer had and didn't like to talk about. She wondered about the details he hadn't revealed.

It looked like she was about to find out.

✧   ✧   ✧

ON THE WAY out of town, Parker and Emily stopped at Caleb Benson's ski shop so Parker could buy a comfortable down jacket, ski pants, and boots for their mini-vacation, things he hadn't brought with him on his trip. Once he shed the shearling jacket and put on the puffer, he felt more like himself than he had in a long time.

Not long after, he and Emily were on their way out of town in her father's more reliable truck. He'd talked her into taking the vehicle on the long ride because it was more practical in case something happened. He'd left James back at the inn, in charge of roofers, electricians, and a host of other repair people working on restoring the place to its former glory. He still didn't know what James planned to do once the work was complete, but for right now, the end game didn't matter.

Emily wasn't stressed about what her father's plans were. She was willing to let him handle the reno and deal with things when it was finished. Parker hoped that by then she'd see how much the inn meant to James and that he was physically and emotionally capable of running it. James just needed a plan.

Then Emily could open her baking business with Harper. If the banks didn't give her a loan, he could. He knew better than to think that she'd just take the money; she was proud like her dad. And Parker, well he'd...

He didn't know what he'd do.

He didn't know what he wanted. Well, he wanted Emily, that went without saying. How he handled the future was a big, open question mark.

Right now he intended to enjoy the present.

They headed out of town, Emily ceding the driving to Parker. She hopped into the passenger seat, shucked her shoes, propped her heavy-sock-covered feet on the dash, and ordered him to drive. With Waze on his cell phone programmed to the Silver Valley Resort, three hours away, he did as she commanded, Queen playing on the radio.

He thought for certain she would pepper him with questions about his love life since Rina, why he hadn't had a lot of females in his life and relationships in his past, but she remained silent, instead tapping her hands to the beat of the music and seeming content in their silence. She was easy to be around. She didn't push him for anything, respecting when he needed to keep things to himself, which should make him happy.

Except he wanted to share parts of himself he'd never given to another woman, which only served to reinforce how deep he was getting with Emily in such a short time.

He drew a deep breath, prepared to discuss the most painful part of his past only to glance over and find her fast asleep. He grinned at the sudden soft snores coming from her side of the car and turned his attention to the road instead.

Three hours later, they arrived at the resort and Parker had to admit it was everything he'd hoped for. The resort looked like a Swiss ski chalet with snowy mountains behind it. Of course, he could also see the runs and the chairlifts behind the lodge near the majestic white-capped mountains, which caused his stomach to cramp. He hadn't been back on skis since the car accident and losing everything, and despite being at a resort, he had no intention of doing so now.

He parked the car and shut the engine before leaning over and stroking a hand down Emily's cheek. "Rise and shine, beautiful. The mountains await."

Long lashes fluttered over her pale skin before she came awake and those beautiful brown eyes focused on him. "Oh my God! I can't believe I slept for all those hours." She jerked to a sitting position, staring out the window before looking back at him.

"I can. We didn't get much sleep last night," he reminded her, gratified to see the blush on her cheeks when she remembered just how they'd spent that time.

"So what do you think at first glance?" She gestured to the building in front of them.

He let her change the subject, finding her embarrassment cute. "It's perfect. I love the rustic look. So warm and friendly feeling."

"I'm so glad. I hoped you'd feel that way. I have a friend I grew up with who is the assistant manager here, which is how I was able to get a room so quickly. They always hold a few over for VIP guests. He did me a favor and is letting us have one. He's going to meet us tomorrow morning to show you around the resort for your retreat."

He nodded. "Perfect."

"Great! Then let's go check in."

They ended up in a room that sold Parker on booking this place for Knight Time Technologies even before he viewed the other amenities. There was a European king-sized bed, the wood furniture was hand painted with beautiful touches and coloring, they had a private balcony and a wood-burning fireplace. Plus, he knew from the brochure he'd picked up downstairs that there were other areas to stay in, chalets and expansion residences that didn't lose the warmth or charm he'd seen so far.

"If I could have conjured the perfect place in my mind, this would have been it," he said after he'd tipped the bellman and he and Emily were alone in the room.

Her smile was contagious. "I'm so glad. I had a feeling this would be perfect."

He pulled her toward him, wrapping her in his arms. "You're perfect."

"I'm not."

"You are. At least in my book." He leaned down and kissed her, not nearly long enough before she started to speak.

"So what do you want to do while we're here? How about skiing? You can show off for me. I'm barely past the beginning stage but I used to be able to hold my own."

She continued to expound on her abilities or lack thereof compared to his, unaware she'd hit a very real nerve. One he'd never truly dealt with. He hadn't had to. Not when he'd had to focus on rehabbing from a serious car accident, grieving Rina, and throwing himself into work for the family company as an escape.

Pulling away, he walked to the window by the balcony he'd been admiring before. He opened the door and stepped outside, not minding the cold, and looked toward the chairlifts and the mountains.

"Parker? What's wrong?" Emily came up behind him. This time she wrapped her arms around him. "Did I say something that upset you?"

125

He blew out a sharp breath. "No. Yes. It's just… I haven't been back on skis since the car accident."

"I'm not sure I follow why."

He felt her warmth against his back and took comfort from her presence. How did he even begin to explain? "I told you about my father not being a good parent. Well, skiing was all I had."

"You had your siblings, and Rina."

She knew him well already.

"I did. But I needed the escape from my home life and skiing was it. The fact that I was good at it was a bonus. Soon it took over and consumed me … in the best possible way. I loved it. The rush down the mountain. The wins, the medals, the endorsements. Hell, even the attention. I ate all of it up."

She squeezed his shoulders, silently urging him to go on.

He felt like the mountains in the foreground were mocking him, but he found the strength to go back to that time. "I took two bronze, and four years later on a bad run, I shattered my knee in the qualifying trials and killed any hope for the Games. Surgery and rehab were a bitch. Sometimes I didn't think I'd get through it."

Rina had been there every step of the way. She'd been his rock. His best friend. But not the woman who consumed his every waking thought like Emily

126

did. And she needed to know who he was and what had brought him to this point. Why he'd taken off from his life in New York so easily.

"Eventually I came back to the sport. I was strong and ready and then came the car accident. I broke my leg and my spirit. After that, I didn't have it in me to rehab again and try and qualify against the younger skiers another four years later. I let my dreams go."

He gripped the railing in front of him and went on. "I figured at that point, I owed Ethan and I needed to go into the family business. I mean, what else was there for me to do?" He exhaled a hard breath. "But I hated everything about my day-to-day life. Eventually I adapted and it became my new normal but it doesn't excite me. I guess that's why it was so easy to decide to take time off when I came here. But to ski? That's another story altogether."

"Hey." She pushed so he'd turn around and face her. "I'm sorry I brought up a sore subject but I'm glad you shared your past with me."

"You're the only one I'd share any part of myself with."

At his words, her eyes darkened with pleasure. "What do you say we christen this huge bed instead?"

Now that was an idea he could get behind. Bending down, he lifted her into his arms. She squealed in delight, winding her arms around his neck as he carried her back into the room.

He slid her to her feet and he studied her. Long blonde hair fell over her shoulder as she began to undress, and the desire to wind the strands around his hand as he pounded into her surged through him. His cock throbbed at the thought and he couldn't tear his gaze away from her as she revealed that silken skin. Somehow he managed to strip his own clothing off at the same time as he watched her.

And then she was standing in front of him, naked, and his breath caught in his throat. Lithe and willowy, she fit him perfectly, her body made for him in every way. For him to worship and devour but right now he just wanted to get inside her and assuage this need she created by just being herself. By listening to him and understanding, she made him feel more than just a physical desire. He wanted to imprint himself on her so she experienced that same deep yearning for him in return.

"God, I want you." He stepped closer and wound his hand around her hair and tugged.

She moaned, clearly enjoying the sensation of pain against her scalp. The sound reverberated in his body, his dick throbbing harder. He pulled her closer and sealed his lips over hers, sliding his tongue over her lips and thrusting into her open, waiting mouth. She kissed him back, the obvious desire inside her matching what he felt for her.

Unable to wait, he turned her around and pushed her face down against the platform bed, the height giving him the right placement and angle for what he had in mind. He reached over to the nightstand, grabbing a condom, ripping the package open, and pulling it on while she waited, ass tipped up, tempting him.

Then he was behind her, nudging her legs apart with his feet. He placed his hand on her back, his cock aligned at her entrance. He trailed his fingers down the bumps of her spine, causing her body to shiver.

He was teasing her, arousing her, working on her anticipation and then he pressed slowly inside. Her body clenched around his dick, pulling him in deeper, and he couldn't wait, gliding out and thrusting back in hard and fast.

"Oh God." She shuddered.

"Fuck." He clenched his teeth and picked up a steady rhythm, taking her hard, knowing from her satisfied cries she was right there with him.

Overwhelmed by the sweet scent he associated with Emily, surrounded by her hot body, and stripped bare by all he'd revealed to her, he slowed down, wanting more than a quick fuck with a woman he was growing to care deeply about.

He slid out and back in, taking care to let her feel

him as he moved. She arched her back, meeting him as he ground into her, their bodies in sync with every thrust of his hips.

It didn't take long before he felt her begin to ripple around him, her body clasping him in tight, wet heat as she came, her scream triggering something inside him, allowing him to let go. His climax took hold, his body stilling as his release exploded, pleasure taking over every part of him, mind, body, and soul.

He collapsed on top of her, his body pressing hers into the mattress long enough for him to catch his breath. He rolled over, then pulled her completely onto the bed. He headed to the bathroom, returning to find her curled under the covers, waiting for him.

He climbed in beside her and she snuggled back into him, where they fell asleep, napping before they awoke for dinner. The hotel boasted a five-star steak house. They enjoyed dinner, and red wine and headed back up to bed, where Parker lit a fire and they cuddled and talked for a while, then made out like teenagers in front of the fire before taking things back to the big bed, where it got even hotter between them.

✧   ✧   ✧

PARKER HAD BREAKFAST in bed with Emily, an intimacy he'd never shared with a woman before. It was a unique experience, one he wouldn't mind repeating. But Emily rushed them out of bed because they had an appointment to tour the resort with her friend, the assistant manager. And since she was doing him a favor, trying to find him a place to hold the corporate retreat, something that would make Ethan happy, Parker pushed himself up and headed for the shower.

A little while later, they were walking through the dark-tiled lobby, furnished with wood accents, by the front desk with the gift and sundry shop to one side.

Emily stopped at the desk. She leaned over, her ass cupped lovingly in a pair of jeans and a white sweater, knee-high tan boots on her long legs. "Hi. I'm Emily Stevens. I'm looking for Colby Mattson. We have an appointment."

An older woman picked up the phone, and a few minutes later, a guy about Parker's age walked around the front desk and headed straight for Emily.

"Em! Come here and give me some sugar! How's my favorite baker?" the man asked. He had dirty-blond hair, wore dark jeans and a cream cashmere sweater, and had a light scruff of beard. Parker grudgingly admitted he was a nice-looking guy who obviously had a thing for Parker's girl.

"Colby!" Emily squealed in delight.

The man pulled her into a very familiar hug that had Parker gritting his teeth before Colby finally put

Emily down. "How's my favorite girl?"

She giggled like an embarrassed schoolgirl and Parker's hand curled into a fist. He wasn't used to this jealous feeling and he didn't like it worth a damn.

"I'm good!"

"Well, I'm glad you're back home where you be- long. Care to tell me about your time in Chicago?"

"Umm–" Her eyes opened wide and she obviously didn't want to share information or go back to that time with Rex.

Not only had Parker had enough of being ignored, nobody was going to push Emily into revealing her past. Not even a so-called old friend.

He stepped forward and pulled her back to him, sliding an arm around her. "Aren't you going to introduce me to your friend?" he asked.

"Oh! I can't believe I forgot," Emily said, a cute blush staining her cheeks.

Colby startled, as if just realizing Parker was there, he'd been so consumed with seeing Emily. Parker figured he could cut the guy some slack. Emily could get a guy to forget his own name. But Colby had planned to give a tour of the lodge and it was time the man remembered and was shown where things stood between the three of them.

"Emily was telling me you and she go way back? You're old *friends*?" Parker pushed, emphasizing the word.

Colby's stare landed on the possessive way Parker's arm wrapped around Emily's waist and his gaze narrowed, coming to rest on Parker's. Clearly he got the message.

"Yes. We went to elementary then middle and high school together. We've kept in touch ever since."

Plenty of time to have made his move, Parker thought to himself. "I'm Parker Knight." He extended his hand and the other man accepted it, his grip a touch too hard and he held on too long.

"Colby Mattson."

He might want a pissing contest but Parker was already the winner here.

"Colby, I told Parker you were going to give us a tour of the resort," Emily, who no doubt was aware of the jealous male undercurrents, said, bringing the subject to why they were here.

Colby nodded. "This place is my pride and joy. We've renovated recently and it has every amenity imaginable while still offering a homey feel. Emily tells me you're looking for a place to hold a corporate retreat?"

"Yes. We'd like to bring a mix of high- and mid-level employees to partake in activities that involve strategizing, enhancing relationships, building morale, as well as giving them time to enjoy themselves."

Colby nodded. "Well, after the tour, if you're inter-ested, we can sit down and discuss packages that included transfers from hotels, excursions to town, ski time, catering, and facilities."

"Actually, once I approve, I'll have someone call you to go over those details. I'm just checking the place out first. I already nixed one too-slick resort that would have my people freezing up instead of relaxing. At a glance, this place is perfect for what I'm looking for. I just need to see the amenities."

"Great." Colby glanced at Emily, who smiled but remained silent, leaving Parker to run his own show. "Let's get started."

For the next two hours, Colby was the perfect host as he explained the amenities of the resort and the reasons it would be perfect for what Knight Time Technologies needed for their retreat. From the town at the bottom of the mountain to the gym at the top floor, the saunas and hot tubs, not to mention the exemplary ski runs that gave Parker a pang of longing, the personal accommodations were perfect. There were two cafes and grills for smaller groups of people, and a larger restaurant that offered American and continental cuisine rated Four Diamonds by AAA.

As for meeting areas for the actual bonding and work time, there were different meeting areas. A conference room for groups of up to twenty-five people to escape everyday demands of work and focus on company strategy, private dining rooms that held groups of up to thirty-five for relaxed dinner meetings, and a larger dining room with views of the village.

"Can I take you two to dinner tonight on the house?" Colby asked when they were finally back in the lobby after a long day of walking the resort.

"That's so sweet of you but it's our last night and we have plans," Emily said before Parker could bark out a rude *no* because all he wanted was to get Emily alone again.

His gaze fell to Emily and softened. "I waited too long."

She blinked in obvious surprise, her face flushing with heat. She really had no idea the effect she had on men, which was one of the many things he found endearing about her.

"Colby—"

He glanced at Parker. "Take good care of her." He extended his hand and Parker took it, liking the man despite the fact that he wanted Emily. They shook in silent understanding, which left Parker shaken, because by no means did he and Emily have any kind of future secured.

AFTER A DELICIOUS dinner that consisted of a light

Chardonnay, an amazing Dover sole, and conversation that was light and fun, Emily now waited for a chocolate soufflé she could not wait to try. It was their last night away and she had enjoyed every minute with Parker. She let all her troubles drift away, she didn't think about the future, and she just let the good feelings of being in the present envelop her.

There was that awkward moment with Colby... She'd had no idea he had any kind of feelings for her beyond friendship. But that was the only thing that marred an otherwise perfect couple of days. She'd checked in with her father and he said everything at the inn was fine and he'd see her when she returned. She couldn't remember the last time she'd been so happy.

"What was that sigh for?" Parker asked, bringing her out of her musings.

She smiled, looking into his amused blue eyes. "I was just thinking how perfect everything has been here. I'm glad we got away. Do you really feel like this is the right place for your retreat?"

"I do. There wasn't one drawback except the distance from the airport, but they accommodate that, too, with drivers and vans. I think even Ethan will love the place."

She nodded. "Me, too. I'm glad."

"So ... I have to ask you something, and if you

136

don't want to talk about it, that's fine, but I noticed how you froze when Colby asked about your time in Chicago. You've told me some things about Rex… Want to tell me the rest before dessert?"

She froze. Again. Parker got that word right. Did she want to tell him? He'd exposed his deepest vulnerability to her, his skiing career being cut short, his fiancée dying in a car crash, his refusal to get back on the mountain. Did she owe him her own truths? More so, did she owe it to herself to unpack the pain and finally unburden herself?

She'd never seen a therapist. Merely come home to take care of her sick mother.

"It's okay. You don't have to say anything." His hand covered hers and he squeezed lightly. "I understand."

But she heard the disappointment in his voice. "I want to. It's just hard. I'm sure you've already put two and two together from meeting Rex and from listening to the things he said. He wanted to change me. He did change me. And I let him." She swallowed hard, picked up a spoon, and twirled it between her hands.

Parker listened in silence, without judgment, and she appreciated that.

"He walked into the bakery I was working in. That was how we met for the first time. We talked. He bought a muffin. He came back the next day. He asked me out for coffee. We started to date. It was a slow insinuation that what I was doing with my life was a waste. I'd gone to culinary school. Why wasn't I using my background to work at a high-end shop? I could be making petit fours and other pastries instead of muffins and cookies. He introduced me to a friend of his and soon I was offered a job at a luxury-type pastry shop in a hotel. At his encouragement, I took it."

She met Parker's gaze. "Go on."

She nodded. "By this time, we were living together. Looking back, I'd changed my clothing choices, my friends, everything that was me." Her hands trembled and she placed them in her lap.

"I was weak at that point. We ran off to Vegas and eloped, which devastated my parents. But he had me so wrapped up in what he wanted, telling me it was what we wanted, that I deprived my parents of their greatest joy, seeing me married." Her voice cracked at the admission. "Then I…"

This was it, she thought. If she told him this, she bared her soul. She swallowed hard. "I got pregnant."

He stiffened, obviously not expecting this part of the story. She didn't look at him. She couldn't, not if she wanted to get through the rest. "I was excited. I wanted the baby. I'm honestly not sure what Rex wanted." To this day, she still couldn't read his reaction … but he was as controlling as ever.

"What made you leave him?" Parker asked gently. "What made you see things for what they were?"

"We had gone to visit friends of his and I'd gone upstairs to the bathroom, and I guess I'd been gone too long so he came looking for me. Which made me uncomfortable. I guess a lot of things did, but I couldn't face them or I'd have to face the mess my life had become along with the fact that I was now trapped because I was pregnant with his baby. We were standing at the top of the steps and arguing."

Parker reached for her hand, pulling it out of her lap and entwining their fingers together. She took so much comfort from his touch and the fact that he was obviously giving her his support.

"I can't remember what the fight was about. Isn't that crazy? I have no recollection whatsoever. Just that we were arguing. I can't remember, either, whether I took the step down and missed or if he reached for me and I jerked away or–" She shook her head, refusing to consider the alternative…

"Or if he pushed you," Parker said through a clenched jaw.

She rolled her shoulders, a tear dripping down her face. "I don't know. I don't want to think so. I just have no idea. I think I don't want to remember. Anyway, I fell down a full long flight of stairs in a center hall colonial. I had cramping immediately. The ambulance took me to the hospital and…" She drew a ragged breath. "I lost the baby."

The waiter chose that moment to walk over with the soufflé. Parker waved the man away and he discreetly stepped back into the shadows.

"Baby, I'm sorry."

Her throat burned and she nodded. "I am, too. But I'm also so grateful that I'm not tied to him forever, and that makes me a horrible human being because that means there's some part of me that's grateful that I lost the baby, too." There. She'd finally said the awful words out loud.

Huge gulping sobs threatened but she held them back somehow, which was a freaking miracle.

Parker reached for her, clearly wanting to pull her into his lap, but she shook her head. If she went to him, she'd fall apart. "I need to finish the story, okay?"

He nodded. "I'm here. Take as long as you need."

"Okay," she whispered. "After… after, I was discharged. Rex went to work the next day. And I packed up the bare minimum, left everything that wasn't the Emily Stevens I wanted to be, and flew home. My mom was going through treatments and I'd planned on coming home to spend time with her anyway. I just came home for good instead. And I threw myself into taking care of my parents."

"And he just let you go? Because that doesn't sound like the man I met," Parker muttered.

She let out a wry laugh. "No. He showed up immediately. Kept talking about how he understood I needed time and I wanted to be there for my mother. He just wasn't hearing me. So I hired a lawyer and I filed for divorce. And he's been making his periodic visits ever since, unwilling to let me go."

Parker scowled but he quickly schooled his expression into one of complete calm. "But time is passing and there is nothing he can do about the divorce becoming legal, right?" He treated her to a reassuring smile, and when he said it, she believed him.

"Right."

He glanced over at the waiter and signaled for him.

The man walked over.

"Box up the dessert and have it sent to the room please?" Parker asked.

"Of course."

Grateful, Emily treated him to a small smile.

"We're going upstairs and I'm going to take care of you, Emily." The dark promise in his voice reverberated through her tortured soul.

After the pain of losing the baby, she'd come home to her sick mom and thrown all her focus into helping her dad take care of her. She hadn't had time to grieve. Parker would let her cry and he'd hold her and be there for her the way no one else had been.

She was coming to rely on him and she didn't know what she would do when he was gone.

Chapter Seven

E MILY HAD BEEN calling her dad for the last half hour on his cell phone and he hadn't answered. Since her mom died, she hadn't been away from home, and she'd just wanted to check on him and let him know they'd be back within the hour. The closer they got to the inn, the more her nervousness increased. Parker didn't say a word. She hadn't mentioned not being able to reach her dad but he couldn't have missed her incessant calling.

She kept herself busy thinking about how gently Parker had handled her after they'd returned to the room last night after she'd told him about losing her baby. No sooner had they entered the suite than he'd kicked the door closed, picked her up in his arms, and walked her over to the bed. He'd sat down and pulled her against him, urging her to let out all the pain she'd been holding in for so long.

And when she was finished, he'd drawn her a bath in the overly large tub, climbing in behind her and pulling her against his hard body, his strong arms

Carly Phillips

cocooning her in warmth and heat, protecting her
against anything that could hurt her. Of course, his
rock-hard erection pressed insistently against her back,
sending spikes of awareness and desire shooting
through her system, until emotional pain was replaced
by physical desire.

If only it was that simple, she thought now. Physical need would be an easy yearning to fulfill. What she
felt for Parker was deeper and reached places inside
her that would be harder to patch up and fix when he
was gone. Even knowing what she'd feel, she'd turned
and straddled him, placed her arms on his shoulders,
her gaze on his, his erection temptingly close to
entering her.

She'd slid her tongue over her bottom lip. "I haven't had sex since before I lost the baby and all my
bloodwork is clean."

He'd expelled a harsh groan. "Tested yearly, and
trust me, it's been a fucking long time for me, too."

"I'm on the pill." It was huge to her, to trust
someone this much, especially this fast but everything
about Parker felt right. She wanted to feel him without
a barrier and, when he was gone, remember everything
about him.

A muscle had ticked in his jaw as he nodded, and
then before she could think, she'd grasped him in her
hand and lowered herself onto his thick cock.

144

What had happened next would stay with her for a good, long time. Their bodies joined, eyes locked, and as they rocked together, if she were one to wax poetic, she'd say their souls spoke to one another. It was that deep and meaningful. She'd felt him take her up and over, knew he'd come at the same time she had, his hands stiffening on her waist as he sealed his mouth over hers.

And afterwards? She'd been shaken by the emotional intensity of their encounter. She'd climbed off him and out of the tub. He'd followed. They'd towel dried and slid into bed, wrapped up in each other, but she was lost in her own thoughts and maybe he was, too, because he left her to them, and they stayed fairly quiet throughout the drive home.

Back in the present, she dialed her father once more. No answer. By the time the inn came into view, she was dying to get out of the truck. Nobody was working on the roof today and the outside of the inn was quiet. Maybe the rain outside explained that, she thought. But it didn't explain why her father wasn't answering her calls.

As soon as Parker pulled into the spot in front of the building, Emily jumped out of the car and ran up the walk to the porch. The front door was unlocked, as it usually was during the day, and she pushed her way in.

"Dad?" she called out. When she got no answer, her stomach twisted and she ran from room to room, still calling out to him, from the family sitting area to the kitchen to his bedroom. When she didn't find him anywhere, she headed back downstairs and ran into Parker.

"I found this in the basement." He held her father's cell phone in his hand.

"Well, that explains why he wasn't answering. Where was it?"

He hesitated before replying. "On the floor next to a ladder that was lying on its side."

"Oh no."

Before she could panic, he took her hand. "Who would he call if he had an accident?"

"He wouldn't call his sister. He wouldn't want to worry her. Let me try the town's doctor. He's one of dad's friends." Her hands shook but she managed to find the number in her phone and dialed.

Robert Carlysle picked up his phone and Emily had her answer. She hung up the phone and met Parker's concerned gaze. "Dad fell off the ladder and hit his head. He needed stitches. He doesn't have a concussion, just a bump on his head. They ran some tests to make sure he didn't get dizzy or have some kind of episode before he fell, and they're waiting on results. I have to get to the hospital."

"*We* have to get to the hospital," Parker corrected her. "And you're upset so I'm going to drive." He placed a hand on her back and led her back out to the truck. "I'll need directions."

She nodded. "Right. Okay." She guided him in the right direction and they headed to the emergency room where her father was, located in the next town over, one slightly larger than Montlake.

Finally, she walked into her dad's room to find him laughing at something Dr. Carlysle, Bob to her father, had said. Laughing. While she'd been in an utter state of panic and worry.

"Dad!"

"Emily, honey! You're back!" He glanced up. He had a bandage on one side of his head but otherwise looked fine.

She rushed over and gave him a hug, panic receding now that she'd seen him for herself.

"Relax, I'm fine. I would have called you once I knew I was okay, but I forgot my phone and I don't have your number memorized," he said sheepishly. He patted her on the back. "Hi, Parker. Thanks for bringing her."

Emily rose to her feet. Her nose was burning and she was doing her best not to cry. She was so damned relieved he was okay, but this had been scary and too close for comfort.

"What were you doing up on a ladder, Dad?"

"The lightbulb died. I was changing it. Accidents happen."

She narrowed her gaze. "Dr. Carlysle, did any of those tests you mentioned come back yet?"

He shook his head. "No, but his blood pressure has been fine since he arrived, he hasn't complained of dizziness or chest pains–"

"I'm telling you, my foot slipped. It could have happened to anyone." He glanced at Parker. "Tell her, son."

His eyes opened wide, a definite deer-caught-in-the-headlights look. There was no way he wanted to take sides, and she shot him an annoyed look for not agreeing with her concern.

"Let me go see if any of the test results are back," Dr. Carlysle said. "Hang tight, James. I'll be back soon." He strode out of the room.

"So, you two, tell me. Did you have a nice time? Parker, was the resort what you need for your company's retreat?"

Emily didn't want to talk about her time away. She wanted to lecture her father about taking unnecessary risks, especially when he was alone in the house with no one around if he fell. But Parker started to expound on the wonders of the lodge. Soon, he and her dad were discussing little touches they could add to rooms at the inn ... and the longer she sat there listening, the more she could feel her blood pressure rising and her head pounding.

The last thing she needed was Parker encouraging her dad. As if this incident hadn't proven what she'd been saying all along – that he wasn't equipped to run the lodge. He should sell the inn, move to Florida, relax, and enjoy his life instead of working. And getting hurt.

"I'm going to take a walk," she said and headed for the cafeteria, needing time to cool off.

"THAT WAS EMILY speak for I'm furious," James said to Parker, as Emily walked out of the room and let the door slam behind her.

"Duly noted." Parker had watched her face as they'd discussed the trip.

She'd been fine until the discussion segued to making small alterations at the inn. The type of changes didn't matter. It was the fact that her father was still emotionally invested in keeping the bed-and-breakfast going and turning it into a viable business that had Emily so upset.

She might have come around to his way of thinking eventually had he not fallen and given her the proof she'd been looking for to back up her feelings that he was too frail to handle things on his own. The fact was, the man wasn't yet sixty years old. Young and nowhere near ready to retire. It was Emily who couldn't see past the death of her mother to accept reality.

"I had a visitor while you were gone," James said. "A representative of a company looking to buy the inn. They're making offers to all the surrounding land owners so they can turn this into a larger corporate resort."

"Same people as before?"

He shook his head. "Different. Pushier. More … determined, I'd say. Either company will destroy the beauty of our small town. We'll lose our image, our brand. It'll become like every other town in America with chain restaurants and stores taking over." He frowned at the idea.

Parker couldn't say he liked it much himself. He scrubbed a hand over his face and groaned.

Even Emily, for all her worry over her father, wouldn't want that to happen to her beloved town. She had dreams of her own she wanted to accomplish here.

As much as he wanted to make her happy and talk her dad into selling to one of these companies interested in the property, he couldn't do it. Not to her and not to her father.

Which meant she was not going to be happy with him. So much for extending their enjoyment now that they were back at her home.

His phone rang from inside his pocket. It wasn't the first time and he couldn't ignore it anymore. He already had declined Ethan's call once while he was away with Emily and ignored him again this morning while driving.

"Excuse me. I need to take this," he said to James and stepped out of the room, walking down the hospital corridor. The hallway was empty and he headed a few feet away.

"Hi, E," he said, answering.

"Fucking finally."

"And I see your mood hasn't improved," he said to his brother.

"How can it when you're still in Bumfuck, Montana?" Ethan asked.

"Colorado," Parker said, rolling his eyes at his brother's dramatics. "You sent me here, remember?" He glanced up to see Emily walking side-by-side with Harper, entering her father's room. He was glad her friend had joined her.

"But I didn't tell you to stay. Or make it your permanent home."

"You're exaggerating. I told you I'm on vacation. I have things here I want to do."

151

And he wasn't ready to leave.

"This is about a woman, isn't it?" Ethan asked, his voice softening. Obviously Sebastian hadn't said anything and Ethan was guessing. The one thing about his older brother, when it came to his younger siblings, he was a softie. The dad they should have had despite his closeness in age.

Parker didn't know how much he was ready to reveal about Emily. There was so much in his head he hadn't yet processed and even more in his heart he hadn't dealt with.

"What if it is?" Parker asked.

"Then you deserve the time to figure it out but I'm not going to let you just disappear." And on that cryptic comment, Ethan said, "I have to get back to work. Talk soon." And he disconnected the call.

Parker wished Ethan would get over Amanda's betrayal and get back to being the man he was. He might have been consumed with work but at least that man had been a semblance of happy.

With a groan, he walked back down the hallway, slowing at the sound of voices coming from James' hospital room.

"Dad, I want you to think more seriously about selling the inn," Emily said.

"Forgetting what I want, which you seem to not want to listen to, I'm not going to be responsible for the cultural change of our town, the destruction of everything that makes Montlake what it is, warm, friendly, your neighborhood where everyone knows everyone."

"I'm not worried about everyone, Dad. I'm worried about you." The distress in Emily's voice was clear and it tore at Parker's heart. "And what about Harper, here? You want her place to become a Starbucks?" James asked.

Parker winced. He was coming to love this small town as much as the people who'd lived here much longer. There was so much good he could do if only his obligations, family and business, weren't in New York. But maybe there was help he could give despite his having to ultimately go home. He needed to think through a strategic business plan without giving anyone false hope.

With that thought tucked away, he knocked and walked into the room, joining the women and James for an afternoon of waiting for tests that ultimately and gratefully came back fine. Emily didn't have much to say to anyone, and sensing she needed time, Parker kept his distance.

He didn't like it, not after how close they'd been all weekend. Not after he'd been so deep inside her body he didn't know where he ended and she began. Not when he'd been in her bare and had a moment of wondering what if he got her pregnant and tied himself to her forever? And no subsequent panic attack occurred. Just a feeling of rightness.

But right afterwards, he'd sensed her withdrawal, a need to take time to herself, and though he was more than willing to be quiet and hold her, he hadn't been willing to go away any farther than that. He'd planned on cajoling her when they arrived back at the inn, but then she'd been obviously unable to reach her dad and things had fallen apart after that.

So yeah, this being ignored sucked about as much as the rest of the choices he would have to make about going home soon.

EMILY WAS ANGRY baking, something she did when she was upset and couldn't sleep. She liked to bake bread because she could give the dough a good pounding and release a lot of frustration that way. She was craving chocolate, and after the day she'd had, she deserved a stress treat, so she was also baking brownies. Her dad was tucked into bed upstairs, well medicated and asleep, and she assumed Parker was in his bedroom. They'd each headed to their own rooms after they'd finally gotten home with her dad, eaten dinner they'd picked up on the way home, and turned in upstairs.

It was awkward between them and she hated it. She smacked the dough for good measure, then began using her favorite marble rolling pin, flattening the dough into a nine-by-twelve rectangle, then rolling it and molding it into a French loaf.

She also hated how much she felt like she was stuck between the proverbial rock and hard place with her dad. She understood how much he wanted to keep and run this inn. She was just truly afraid it was too much for him, and a big part of her was afraid of losing him the way she'd lost her mom.

She repeated the process with more dough. A glance at both loaves, and she added a few diagonal cuts with a knife, then placed them on a greased baking sheet, leaving them to rise.

Her thoughts immediately returned to her dad. Her fears. It didn't help that she'd been mired in grief over her baby at the same time her mother had passed away. It'd been difficult to separate the two losses. She was still getting over them both. So yes, maybe she overreacted with her dad. Maybe she was irrational. But feelings were feelings, right?

She blew out a long breath and turned her attention to the brownies, which she already had in a bowl. They just needed to be poured into the pan and slid into the oven. She'd been at this awhile.

Then she'd lick that bowl clean. She wouldn't have

solved her problems but she'd have eaten chocolate … and that was something, right?

✧ ✧ ✧

PARKER LISTENED IN vain for any noise coming from Emily's room but he didn't hear anything. He didn't for a second think she'd gone to sleep. She had as much on her mind as he did. Maybe more.

He knocked on her door, and when she didn't answer, he headed downstairs to the second most obvious place to find her. Sure enough, she was muttering to herself in the kitchen while stirring what looked like chocolate in a large bowl.

He pulled up a stool and slid onto it, watching her while she worked. He had no doubt she'd heard and seen him come in. So he took in the unbaked loaves rising on the counter and he inhaled the delicious smell of chocolate.

"My mother used to bake." The words were out before he could even think them. He hadn't even realized he'd had the sensory memory but it warmed him inside. "She liked to include me and my brothers when we were little."

Emily stilled in her mixing, her soft gaze coming to his. "What did she make?"

"Well, brownies in a pinch, of course." He nodded toward her bowl. "And Snickerdoodles. Those were my favorite." He smiled, almost able to smell the cinnamon.

"I like the dreamy look on your face."

"It isn't often I'm thrown into a good memory of my mom," he admitted.

More often than not, he thought about the bitter ones of his dad and his lack of attention, his many wives, and losing the one parent who loved him unconditionally.

"Do you know the key ingredient that differentiates a Snickerdoodle from a sugar cookie?" she asked.

He shook his head. "Can't say that I do." That memory escaped him.

"Cream of tartar. It's a leavening agent that gives the cookie its signature tangy flavor and chewy texture."

"She made them every Christmas," he said, hearing his own wistful tone. "We left them out for Santa."

Emily smiled at his memory. "I'll make them for you one day if–" She shook her head.

If you're still here went unsaid.

"Can I take this to mean you're not mad at me anymore?" he asked, leaning in on one arm.

She poured the brownie mix into the pan and sighed. "I was never mad at you. At first I was just scared to death. Then I was frustrated with Dad and the situation. You being here, supporting his dream

157

doesn't help. But I'm not angry at you."

The heaviness in his chest eased. But he was going to throw her an even more difficult question. He wasn't sure if he expected an answer, and given he didn't know if he could answer in return, it wasn't exactly fair.

"Okay then, good. What about before we came back? Are you still running from what we felt?"

She'd stuck a chocolate-covered finger into her mouth, and at the question, her eyes opened wide. The question had been bad timing on his part because his dick hardened at the sight of that finger in her mouth. He wanted her lips wrapped around his cock.

But they had important things to discuss. "Running?" she asked on a squeak.

He pushed himself to standing and strode around the island, coming up to her and pushing her back against the counter. "Running," he confirmed. "Not physically but emotionally."

"I can't let myself get too attached to you, Parker. You're leaving. Sooner not later. Just because we don't discuss it doesn't make it not true. I need to protect myself."

Her words sliced through him because they were true. Because he hated them. Because she was right and he didn't want her to be. So he did the only thing he could do in the moment.

"But we have now." He reached for the bowl and slid his finger through the chocolate.

Then, pulling up her tee shirt, he found her braless, which worked for what he had planned. He coated both of her nipples with the mixture, smearing it over the buds and her areolas, then dipped his head and began to lick her clean.

He suckled on the sweet treat, pulling the beaded tip into his mouth and releasing it with a pop, swirling his tongue around and around until one side was clear. Afterward, he turned his attention to the other side, giving it the same treatment, reveling in the soft sighs of pleasure and outright moans of delight that came from the back of her throat as he aroused her with his mouth and tongue.

Her hips rocked from side to side along with his licks and caresses, and he pressed his hips against hers, grinding himself against her sex. She hooked one leg around his thigh and thrust herself against him, rubbing into him until she came on a cry. He captured the sound in his mouth, and dammit if he didn't come, too, in his pants like he was fucking sixteen years old.

Cheeks flushed, she slid off him. "Well, that was something." She laughed. "Did we really just…?"

"Yeah. We did."

Grinning, he walked over to the sink and turned on the water. "You wash your hands. I'm running to the bathroom. Then I'll come back and help you clean up the mess in here."

He walked out and she rinsed off her hands and got the baked goods into the oven. Parker returned and they took care of the baking tins and flour that was everywhere, cleaning up and talking while the bread and brownies baked, falling into bed late and sleeping in the next day.

Together.

THE NEXT MORNING, her baking for Harper's shop complete, Emily rushed around the kitchen, finishing up last-minute details before she could leave to go into town. Harper had texted her that she needed to talk to her – alone – and it was important. So she wanted to get moving.

But it was her father's first morning after his fall and she needed to see for herself that he was okay. He still had the white bandage on his head but he seemed to be mobile and doing well. He tipped back his coffee mug and looked ready to rise.

"Dad, don't get up. I'll get you more coffee," Emily said, grabbing his mug and walking over to the Keurig.

"She knows I'm not an invalid, right?" James asked Parker, who sat beside him at the kitchen table, sipping his own cup in silence.

"She's worried about you after your fall. Humor her," Parker suggested.

He was right. She was concerned. But that didn't mean they needed to talk about her like she wasn't in the room.

"*She* is right here and doesn't appreciate being talked about in the third person." After pushing the brew button, she finished wrapping the last of her muffins she needed to take over to Harper's for the breakfast rush.

"Do you know how much easier your baking routine would be if you'd just look into leasing the space next door to Harper's Coffee? No more loading up the car, no more getting up extra early because you only have one oven…"

"Dad, really? You want to have this discussion now?" She braced her hands on the counter and faced her father. "I'm still working on getting you to see reason about yourself and this inn."

He rolled his eyes. "I am seeing reason. I took a tumble anyone in my position could have taken. Should I have waited until someone was home to climb the ladder? Yes. I won't make that mistake again. Lesson learned." He rose from his seat and walked over to the coffee machine and took the cup she'd forgotten, added milk, and took a sip. "See? Perfectly capable of doing things for myself."

She blew out a breath. "I need to get into town. I'm glad you're feeling better, Dad. Really. If you need anything–"

"I'm here. You didn't want help taking your muffins to town, so I'm hanging here with James."

"We're going to discuss what remains to be done on renovations," her father said, clearly excited and pleased with himself.

Parker shook his head. "Not helping," he muttered and she couldn't help but chuckle under her breath. Her dad was a stubborn man.

And she didn't wonder where her own personality had come from.

"Which reminds me, you need to look into hiring a decorator to redo the inside of the place. We're going to change it all up and I want you to feel like you're picking what you want," her father said, sipping from his mug.

"Why do I feel like you're ignoring me?" she asked.

"Maybe because I am? This is happening," he informed her.

She knew when to give up the fight at least for now. "Okay, you two. See you later."

Later, after the morning rush, during which Emily helped out because Harper was short-staffed, they were able to sit down at a quiet table to talk.

"Whew. That was a busy morning," Emily said.

"It was. And I'm grateful for it. Which is why what I have to tell you is so important." Harper fidgeted in her seat and it was obvious she had something on her mind.

"Talk to me."

"Okay." She looked around, obviously making sure they were alone. "My landlord called. He got an offer. Not just on the store we have our eye on but he offered to buy out my lease because they want to purchase the entire block." Harper's eyes opened wide. "I couldn't believe what I was hearing."

Neither could Emily and her stomach twisted painfully. She'd been putting off this decision because she could. Because the perfect store was there waiting for her to come around or not. "What did you tell him?"

"That the coffee shop is my life and I had no desire to walk away. I said I had a lease he couldn't break and that I'd get back to him about an offer on the place next door. Oh hell, I broke down and begged him not to sell. I don't want a landlord who's going to make my life hell and evict me!"

Emily pinched the bridge of her nose, a headache beginning to form there. "What can we do?"

"Don't be mad."

She narrowed her gaze. "What did you do?"

"I made us an appointment with the bank," Harper

said on a rush. "In" – she glanced at her phone – "fifteen minutes so we could apply for a small-business loan."

Emily bit down on the inside of her cheek. "Don't you already have a small-business loan?"

"Yes, but I'm making my payments. Look, we have to try. This is our dream, right? Well, it's going to dissolve in front of our eyes if we don't at least attempt to do something to stop it."

Knowing this was it, that she either jumped on opportunity or regretted it forever, she looked at her best friend and nodded. "Okay. Let's go apply for a loan. I have to warn you, I don't have any collateral."

"Goodwill goes a long way in small towns. I hope," Harper muttered, grabbing her hand and pulling her out of her chair.

They headed to the bank to meet with the loan officer. Emily didn't leave overly optimistic but she knew she'd tried. She had statements and paperwork she had to forward to them and she decided to hold on to hope.

But she swore Harper to secrecy. She didn't want to tell Parker she'd applied for a loan. She knew he was wealthy and he clearly had the money to fund the inn. For sure, he'd offer her a similar deal to the one he'd made with her father. She didn't want to owe him money.

It wasn't that she didn't trust him. It wasn't that she put him in the same category as Rex or thought he'd try to control her even if she did take a loan from him. It was that she didn't want him to feel like he had to keep propping up her family because he felt bad for them. Or because he liked her. Or was sleeping with her. He wasn't a bank. And that was that.

So she hugged Harper and they parted ways, fingers crossed, and promised to keep in touch and get the needed information to the bank.

Chapter Eight

EMILY WAS HOLDING something back. Parker wouldn't outright call it lying. She was too sweet for that. But she was vague about her morning and she'd been gone longer than a typical time delivering her goodies to Harper, even if he included her helping out and talk time with her best friend.

Then there was the noise coming from her father's study … it sounded like a fax machine running, and since James was busy with the people who would be replacing the windows at the inn, meeting at their warehouse, he wasn't the one using it. He'd slipped out while Emily was in town so she couldn't hover and insist he wasn't up to driving. The doctor had said he could do what he felt he could handle.

And now, when she wasn't in the office with the door closed, she was on the computer.

"Everything okay?" he asked from his seat on the sofa in front of the fireplace.

She glanced over, looking up from where she'd been staring at the screen. "Sure is!" she said too brightly.

He narrowed his gaze but let her have her privacy.

He was about to turn his attention to his life and when he was going to go back to New York, something he didn't want to face, but he couldn't stay in Colorado forever. He glanced over at Emily, bent over her laptop, blonde hair falling in her face, covering her expression, and his heart gave a kick in his chest.

He wasn't ready to go.

But Ethan would need him back soon. He couldn't just check out of life indefinitely.

The sound of a car door slamming startled them both and they jumped at the noise. "Expecting anyone?" he asked her.

She shook her head. "Maybe Dad's back early." She jumped up from her seat at the same time the front door opened and her asshole almost-ex walked in like he owned the place.

Parker stood, pissed, before the man opened his mouth and said a word. If it were up to him, he didn't care how small this town was, the front door to this place needed to be locked.

"Rex. What are you doing here?"

"At some point, aren't you going to admit you're happy to see me?"

Parker coughed. "Is your head really that far up your ass?" Parker wasn't going to start out being nice.

Rex scowled at him. "You're still here?"

Folding his arms across his chest, Parker grinned. "Haven't left."

Parker took in the other man's outfit. He'd been in a suit during his last visit and he'd learned his surroundings because now Rex was wearing a pair of jeans, pressed like Parker's had been when he arrived, which Parker had quickly realized didn't fly out here in Colorado. Relaxed comfort was key and Parker had adapted accordingly, wanting to fit in where Emily lived and, in doing so, finding more of himself.

He had a hunch that Rex's change of clothes had everything to do with the fact that Rex now had competition for Emily and he wanted to make the point that he, too, could adapt. Rex was full of shit, Parker thought. He only wanted Emily to fall for his crap long enough to get her back to Chicago and begin his subtle brainwashing all over again.

Rex glanced around the inn. "The roof looks good," he noted. "Better than all the construction going on last time. Should help you raise the sale price," he said, looking around.

"What makes you think we're going to sell?" Emily asked. "This is my family's legacy. You're out of your mind if you think we're going to hand it over to developers to destroy the beauty of the inn and the town."

Parker wondered if she heard her own words or realized the import of what she'd just admitted. She might fight her father's desire to keep this place alive and vital, fear for his health driving her, but she loved it as much as he did. She loved the town. She wasn't going to let it be destroyed.

As he thought about Rex's words, Parker narrowed his gaze. "What would make you even ask such a thing?"

The other man shrugged off the question. "People who renovate the old often do it with resale value in mind," Rex said to Parker, as if he were an imbecile for not knowing those things himself. "I just assumed."

That let Parker smirk. "You know what they say about people who assume."

Rex frowned and looked away from him. "Emily, can we talk privately? I have news you're going to want to hear," he said, sounding excited by whatever he had to tell her.

"You can say anything you have to in front of Parker. We have no secrets." She didn't glance Parker's way and he knew for sure they had one. He just didn't know what it was yet. He wasn't all that concerned, though he wished she'd trust him with her secrets since she clearly had that trust when it came to dealing with her almost ex-asshole.

"Fine. Guess what? I spoke to the owners of La Paris Patisserie in downtown Chicago and they want to hire you as soon as possible. It's such a prestigious opportunity. Think of the doors that would open for you after time there," he said, obviously very pleased with himself.

Parker didn't know Chicago pastry shops well but he assumed this was a premiere one. He also knew Emily had no desire to move back to Illinois, reunite with this jerk, or bake anything other than what she was doing now. None of this, Rex was willing to accept.

"You don't listen." Taking Parker by surprise, Emily had walked up to Rex and begun poking him in the chest, in time with each word, making her point. "We're over, Rex. I live here now. I love it here. I love baking muffins and wearing sweats and yoga pants. I like pulling my hair into a messy bun–" which she'd done at some point and Parker hadn't noticed but she looked sexy. "I love my life without you in it!" she yelled at him.

Parker wanted to applaud her but refrained. No point in riling up Rex any more than he already was, if the red stains on his cheeks were any indication of his fury.

"You don't know what you're missing out on," he said, reaching for her.

Before she could even step out of the way, Parker was there, gripping the man's wrist in his stronger grasp. "You don't touch her. Ever."

He glared at Parker, looking ready to throw a punch, but being smart, the man thought better of it, wrenched his hand back, and stepped away.

He turned to Emily. "I'm offering you the world. You really are going to regret turning me down."

She grew pale but she drew her shoulders back and met his gaze, making Parker proud. "Not a chance in hell. Now get out." She held on to her bravery as Rex glared, turned, and stormed out of the house, slamming the door behind him.

Her shoulders caved but Parker clapped, something he'd been wanting to do as he watched her handle Rex. "You told him, baby. Good job."

"Do you think that's the end of it? That he got the message?"

Parker gave it some thought. "I wish I knew. I think you should let your lawyer know he would have grabbed you if I wasn't here. Let him know there was an imminent threat. But he didn't hit you or try to. He reached for you. I doubt it's enough to get you a restraining order but anything you document could only help if you need it in the future."

She agreed, walked over to the phone, and called Harper's brother, Gary, her attorney in the divorce, spoke to him for a while, and hung up, facing Parker. "You're right. I need to be able to tell the court that Rex hurt or threatened to hurt me." She shivered at that and he reached out, pulling her close. "If I'm not in imminent danger of further threats or abuse if the order isn't issued, there's nothing more we can do."

He held her tight. "I can get a bodyguard–"

"No. He's not a threat. He's like a little boy who is upset he didn't get his way. I just want to forget about him. Put it all behind me. Maybe now he won't be back." She wriggled out of Parker's embrace. "I'm fine. I'm not going to let Rex get to me." She walked back to her computer and sat down, pressed a few keys, and waited for the screen to boot up again.

Well, okay then, Parker thought. If she wanted to move on, they'd move on. "What are you working on?" he asked.

Her eyes opened wide, her expressive face totally showing him he'd caught her unprepared on that question. "Umm, I'm going to start looking at wallpaper." She lied.

He shrugged. "Guess you're accepting the inn is happening and your father is running it?"

Her cheeks flushed. "I'm going to make sure he has enough help that he doesn't run himself ragged, that's what I'm going to do," she muttered. "But to answer your question, yes. I've accepted it."

173

He couldn't help but grin. "For the record, I think it's the right thing to do. This place makes your father happy. So what if it reminds him of your mother's dream? He gets enjoyment out of fulfilling it." He rolled his shoulders. "It's beautiful if you ask me."

"What is?" She turned, her arm on the back of the kitchen chair as she faced where he sat on the sofa in the great room.

"A love like theirs," he said wistfully, knowing that he'd found it here in Colorado. With Emily.

The notion should shock him but he'd been building toward this deep relationship from the start. He'd never been hit so hard or fast by a woman, her impact on him had been that strong. Hell, *she'd* kept him here although he'd never let on it was because of her. She'd have run far and fast. She'd needed time to get to know him. To trust him. To see he wasn't the city boy she'd first pegged him as, not in a bad way, at any rate. And he hoped that now she knew him as well and as deep as he knew her.

As he thought about his feelings, his heart, the one she owned, pounded hard and fast in his chest. This wasn't an easy revelation for him to come to or accept, and not just because they lived on opposite sides of the country. What had love shown him within his family?

Ethan had given Mandy everything he could of

himself and she'd betrayed him. His father went through women like others went through Kleenex. But his mother had loved his father, a little voice reminded him. And had she lived, who knew what kind of marriage they would have had. He didn't have bad memories of his dad from his early years. Had he been so devastated by losing the love of his life that he'd ruined what had come after for his children?

Parker would never know. He'd never sit down and have that kind of conversation with Alexander Knight. He wasn't the type of man for that. Not now, anyway.

But these feelings inside Parker for Emily were clear. Protective, warm, loving.

Dammit.

"I know exactly what you mean," she said, bringing him back to thoughts of her parents' marriage and the love they'd shared. "My father loved my mother and he loves to be surrounded by things she loved." Emily sighed, her soft gaze on Parker's.

And for a brief second, her heart was in her eyes before she shuttered the look and buried herself in the computer screen again. Because what could she do? She knew the facts as well as he did. She lived here, had roots here. She wasn't a city girl. She'd tried it and it hadn't worked out for her, and he had a hunch, although it had much to do with Rex, she wouldn't want to try Manhattan.

And he wouldn't ask her to.

Which left him exactly where he'd started.

Nowhere.

✦　✦　✦

"DAMMIT, APPARENTLY WHEN they're turning you down, it doesn't take a bank long at all to make a decision!" Harper called out as she stormed into the inn a few days later.

Parker's eyes opened wide.

James' did as well.

Emily glared at her friend, who glanced around at the full house and winced. "Oops. I'm so sorry, Em. I didn't even think, I was just so upset."

A small shrug belied how obviously upset Emily was. Her entire expression had fallen. Both she and Harper looked beside themselves.

"Tell me what's going on," Parker said, his gaze more on Emily's than Harper's. "I've known for days you were hiding something, so out with it."

Harper looked to Emily for belated permission and she nodded. She went on to explain about the offer her landlord had gotten from a big corporation to buy the land that housed both the coffee shop and the empty space next store, along with his offer to buy her out of her lease.

"So we thought, let's at least try to fulfill our dream before it all goes up in smoke."

"That's the same company who recently made me an offer here," James said. "It's like they want to take over the town." He shook his head. "That's not something we can allow." He pounded his hand on the table, his anger evident.

"Did they say why they turned us down?" Emily asked.

Harper nodded. "I'm overextended and you—"

"Have no credit. Got it."

Parker's heart broke for her.

"I should go," Harper said, regret in her tone. "I'm really sorry again, Em."

"It's not your fault." She hugged her friend. "I'll call you later. Don't agree to let him buy you out of your lease. One step a time, all right?"

Parker rose to his feet. "We'll get this worked out," he assured Harper. "And when we're ready for real discussion, we'll all sit down and—"

"No!" Emily jumped up from her seat on the couch, going from accepting to panicked in a heartbeat. "This is exactly what I didn't want to happen."

"She'll call you," he promised Harper.

No sooner had Emily's friend walked out than James rose to his feet. "I'm going to watch some television in my room," he said, disappearing obviously so they could be alone to talk.

Emily turned to face him. She was wearing a pair of jeans and a sweatshirt, the front cut into a low vee, and he couldn't tear his gaze from the cleavage he'd tasted so thoroughly last night. They'd spent every night since they'd been home from their trip in his bed, gathering up every minute of time together they could without discussing the obvious ticking clock.

Parker waited until James was upstairs before turning his attention back to the situation at hand. He strode over to the sofa. "Sit."

Frowning, she did as he said.

He settled in beside her, easing in close. He wasn't about to give her any wiggle room, physically or otherwise, then picked up her hand in his. "We never discussed money," he said quietly.

Her face contorted in horror. "Because it's none of my business what you have."

He couldn't stop the grin that followed. "And that is one of the things I love about you, Emily Stevens."

❖　❖　❖

AT PARKER'S WORDS, Emily's mouth opened in shock.

Placing his hand beneath her chin, he closed it again. "You can't be surprised.

She swallowed hard and it wasn't easy. She had no moisture left in her mouth. "I can be floored that you said it out loud."

He groaned, tipping his head and leaning it against hers.

"What I feel and what I can ultimately do about it are two very different things. And that's why I don't even want you to say the words back."

But they were there, threatening to spill out. Of course she loved him. If it was possible, she'd loved him on sight, even when she'd thought she hated him. She couldn't even list the reasons but she tried. He was everything she hadn't known she was looking for. Her kind, protective, loving, generous city boy. She should be happy.

But the meaning behind all of his words caused her heart to race in panic. Yes, she knew he'd leave … eventually. And she knew eventually was becoming sooner rather than later. But she wasn't ready. She loved him, too.

"But that's not what we're discussing now."

Good, she thought, her heart rate slowing. A re-prieve. She needed one along with time to catch her breath. This amazing man loved her and that was something she'd always have … even if she couldn't have him. She glanced down and realized she'd been gripping his hand in hers.

She nodded in understanding. The more painful talk would come soon enough.

"Back to the bank loan. Look at the lengths you went to in order to hide the fact that you tried to get a bank loan from me. I admire your pride and determination to go it alone but—"

She glanced away. "I'm not going to be your charity case, Parker. You can't support my whole family."

He drew in a deep breath. "My family is ... well, let's just say that buying the real estate out at whatever price the corporation offered isn't a problem. That would remove all temptation from the landlord and let you rent for market price."

"With you as my landlord." She bit down on her lower lip.

"I know how you feel about it but I can't think of another way to make sure Harper keeps her shop. The new landlord is going to make her life difficult if she stays because he clearly wants to gut and build. So he'll make it as hard as he can for her to stay without crossing the line of being illegal."

"Oh my God. I didn't even think of that. Harper said it would be hard to have a new landlord but..."

"Listen, all Harper will be doing is paying me. I'll hire a company out here to keep the place in working order so you're not having issues or problems. As for the joint business, I'll float you two a small-business loan. You give me a business plan ... show me what you have in mind, what you need financially, and we'll go from there."

Tears filled her eyes. "I didn't want to have to do this but ... I don't know how to thank you. I fought Dad on the inn, Harper on the business ... I think I was just afraid of relying on a man for my happiness."

She threw her arms around his neck and he pulled her against him, burying his face in her fragrant hair. Yeah, his dick hardened and he wanted her, but he'd made her happy and that meant so much more to him than sex.

As she ran off to call Harper, Parker leaned back against the couch and groaned. He'd funded the renovation on the inn and now he was going to make an offer on a piece of land/shopping center in Montlake, Colorado. He hadn't intended to tie himself to the town but that was exactly what he'd done.

But the strongest of the roots he'd be leaving here was his heart.

FOR PARKER, THE next few days were filled with meeting Harper's landlord, calling Parker's money manager to transfer funds and liquidate enough money to handle the transaction to purchase the land, his lawyer to begin working on a sales contract, and helping Emily and Harper construct a business plan for their addition and construction to turn both shops into one.

The landlord, who was a longtime resident of the town, had been relieved by Parker's blunt approach, letting the landlord know Parker wanted only to save the integrity of the town and the shops that existed here. The man hadn't wanted to sell but he'd been unable to find a way to turn down the amount of money the corporation had offered when it would enable him and his wife to live comfortably for the rest of their lives. Parker's solution solved his problem.

As for Emily, once she'd wrapped her head around the fact that her plans were actually happening, she had thrown herself into the project one hundred percent. He enjoyed working with the women, seeing their enthusiasm, and offering his help and guidance where he could.

Knight Time Industries offered smart homes and offices, and he could offer them smart light switches and thermostats and generally give them state-of-the-art equipment for little to no extra cost, just because he wanted to. They also discussed green technology and he'd see what could be incorporated in the older building. Emily and Harper were enthralled by the notion. Sure, it was excessive in a small town with a small business but why not start somewhere? Besides, he wanted Emily to have the best and he could give it to her.

He was busier than he'd been since arriving in town and he liked the energy he felt along with the sense of accomplishment he experienced in getting things done.

✦　✦　✦

EMILY WAS ALONE at the inn. Parker had gone out for a walk and she'd passed on joining him. Her dad was out for lunch with a friend, a break he'd earned after supervising so many workmen and areas of the inn. They had a new boiler, AC unit, roof, and now he wanted to renovate the kitchen and redo the rooms. He left it to her to pick out the appliances, counter-tops, and cabinetry because those items were in her wheelhouse – his words – and the budget she'd been given was more than generous, enabling her to buy top-of-th-line everything.

She couldn't get over how Parker had basically funded the entire thing... She would repay the money if it killed her but she'd never be able to express her gratitude in any way that would show what it meant to her, the fact that he'd saved her family's legacy and allowed her to achieve her ultimate dream.

She glanced at the wallpaper books open on the table, trying to decide on how to handle the rooms. Did she go with unique paper in each or a theme for the overall inn? Or did she give it up and hire a decorator as Parker had suggested when she'd worried she didn't have the eye for the task?

A knock sounded at the front door, which was unusual in and of itself. Everyone in town knew to just walk in during the day. Even Rex just showed up at will.

She rose to her feet and walked toward the door. "Come in!" she called out just as the door pushed in and an unfamiliar man stepped inside.

He wore a rumpled suit that indicated he'd been traveling for a while to get here, with a trench coat hanging from his arm. He had long, scraggly dark hair, blue eyes that reminded her of someone, she couldn't place who, and a scruffy beard. All in all, he was a handsome, if angry-looking, man.

"Can I help you?" she asked.

"I'm looking for my brother. Parker Knight."

Oh, wow. From what Parker had told her, Sebastian was the fun, easygoing brother, which meant this had to be Ethan. The perpetual grump, according to Parker.

"Hello, welcome. I'm Emily Stevens." She held out her hand.

"Ethan Knight." He shook it, his steady gaze assessing her from head to toe. He was definitely measuring her worth and she was uncomfortable.

"Parker went for a walk but if you come in, he

should be back soon. Here. Let me hang up your jacket." She reached for his trench coat.

He let her take it and she hung it in the front hall closet. "Welcome to the Ruby Rose Inn." She smiled.

He didn't.

"It's named after my mom," she said, rambling in the wake of his silence. "Umm, can I get you something to drink? Iced tea? Soda? Water?"

"Water is fine, thank you."

He followed her into the kitchen and took in the array of books spread open on the table.

"I'm sorry. I'll clean up so you can sit comfortably. I wasn't expecting company."

"So this place doesn't have any guests at the moment?" he asked, looking around.

She bit the inside of her cheek. "We're currently renovating. We'll take people who are stuck, like Parker when he showed up, because we wouldn't turn anyone away." She didn't mention that she'd done just that to his brother on his arrival, afraid of everything he'd seemed to represent.

"I see. Did my brother look like a perfect target to take advantage of?"

She'd just reached the refrigerator and had been about to pull out a bottle of cold water. "I'm sorry, what?"

"I asked if you took one look at my brother, spot-

185

ted wealth, and immediately sunk your hooks into him?"

The blood drained from her head and she grew dizzy as she forced herself to meet Parker's brother's gaze. The man thought she was a gold digger, and she had to admit, given all Parker had done for her, things didn't look good.

"Jesus Christ, Ethan. Shut your fucking mouth or I'll shut it for you," Parker snapped, startling Emily with his sudden presence. "Now apologize to Emily before I have to do something to my older brother that we'll both later regret."

"Parker, I didn't hear you come in. Your brother's here," she said for no good reason when it was obvious. "Don't fight with him over me. He's your family."

The sad thing was, as the protective father figure in the family, she couldn't blame him for looking down his nose at Emily considering the amount her family had taken from Parker. And no matter what Ethan thought or felt about it now, she couldn't stop the money transfer and land purchase. It was done and she'd pay Parker back as planned.

Parker strode over and slid his arm around her waist, pulling her to his side. "Emily, don't listen to him. He doesn't know anything except the conclusions he's drawn with very little information and even less common sense." He sounded pissed at his sibling.

But Emily wasn't going to allow it. "I can't say he's all wrong about those conclusions. It looks bad, doesn't it?" She shook her head sadly, never having anticipated meeting Parker's family, or the brother he adored hating her on sight.

It hurt, she admitted, her stomach in knots. Even if they didn't have a future, she'd have wanted to make a good impression on the man Parker obviously loved and idolized for all he'd done for the family. The last thing she wanted to do was come between siblings.

"So this is the way it is? You two are together." Ethan's gaze encompassed how Parker had protectively drawn her against him.

She wriggled out of his grasp. "I'll leave you two alone," she said. Wrapping her arms around herself, she walked out of the kitchen, head held high.

All she'd done, she reminded herself, was borrow money from a wealthy man who'd offered it freely and willingly. She hadn't asked. And she was sure Parker would set his brother straight. But it didn't negate the bad taste in her mouth over the encounter that only served to remind her that not only did she and Parker live on opposite sides of the country, they came from two very different worlds.

Chapter Nine

PARKER WATCHED EMILY go, her shoulders back, holding on to the pride that Ethan had tried to strip from her. "You asshole. Where do you get off showing up here and talking to the woman I love that way?" Parker shouted at his brother.

Probably for the first time ever.

His family didn't call Parker Switzerland for no reason. He kept to himself, didn't take sides and remained neutral, and was usually mellow. Now Ethan knew what it took for him to explode.

"Well?" he asked when Ethan didn't answer immediately.

"Well what?" Ethan shot back. "Our lawyer mentions you're buying commercial property in Colorado, the financial guys send over statements showing huge transfers of funds, what the fuck am I supposed to think?"

Muscles tensed in Parker's shoulders. "That I know what I'm doing, for one thing. And so much for attorney-client privilege," he muttered under his breath. "Look, Ethan, I'm telling you and not for the first time that I'm an adult. I know how to run my life. You need to mind your own damned business."

Ethan braced his hands on the counter, ignoring the wallpaper books open everywhere. "Are you telling me that you're not giving out money like it's candy to this woman and her family? Just like you're doing with Rina's parents?"

Parker scrubbed a hand over his face and groaned. "That's not fair. They're two completely different situations, and if you'd pull your head out of your grieving ass and pay attention to what I'm saying, maybe you'd understand instead of jumping to conclusions."

Sliding out a chair, Ethan sat down and faced Parker. "I'm listening."

Parker drew a deep breath and decided to meet his brother halfway. "I admit that I paid the Londons out of sheer guilt that I lived and their daughter didn't. I can even, with time away, say it's been a mistake and I will handle it and it'll end. But what I'm doing here in Colorado is different."

"How? You showed up, met people in need, next thing you know you're fixing the problem."

Parker shook his head. "It's a hell of a lot more complicated than that."

Ethan met his gaze and said, with a shake of his

head, "Right. You fell in love."

"You know what?" Parker rose from his seat. "You're being a prick. Maybe Mandy betrayed you, cheated on you, and stole from the company, but not every woman is like her and I'll be damned if I'll let you paint Emily with the same brush. I'm sorry you came all this way but you can just turn around and take your ass and shitty attitude back home."

Ethan reached out a hand. "Come on, Parker. You know I'm just looking out for you."

No, he was butting in as usual. "I have nothing more to say to you." He stormed out of the kitchen and headed upstairs to find Emily, hoping he could undo some of the damage his brother had done.

EMILY SAT ON her bed and attempted slow-breathing exercises to calm herself down. She was beyond hurt and insulted that Parker's brother treated her the way that he had. The man didn't know her at all. Although, she could see how, on paper, it looked like she was taking advantage of his brother. She'd been concerned about doing that from the beginning. Still, she and Parker had been nothing but honest about her feelings regarding borrowing his money. And that's what she and her father were doing. Borrowing. They had the paperwork to prove it.

She sighed, leaning back against the pillows, hating how she could hear the raised voices coming from downstairs. Parker shouldn't be arguing with his sibling over her. She knew how much he loved Ethan, how Ethan was like the father he should have had, and she didn't want to come between them.

A knock sounded on the door, coinciding with silence from the main floor. She opened the door to Parker.

"My brother's an asshole," he said without preamble.

She sighed. "He's got a point, though, doesn't he? You're shelling out money to us like we're a charity case."

Anger flared in his eyes. "I'm *lending* money. There's a difference. And I'm investing in real estate, which is a smart thing to do. All of which are decisions I'm free to make without my brother's approval, I might add."

Leaning against the door, she met his gaze.

"Can I come in? I want to explain a few things to you, which might help you to understand why Ethan jumped to the conclusions he did. Nothing will make what he said to you acceptable, but there are some things you should know."

She stepped aside so he could enter. With nowhere else to sit, they settled on the bed facing each other.

"Ethan is jaded to say the least." Parker met her gaze as he spoke. "His wife died eight months ago. After that he found out she was cheating on him and stealing from our company. He's obviously distrusting of everyone and everything right now."

"Particularly women," Emily said, understanding a little more where the man had been coming from. She even felt bad for him, losing his wife and being blindsided by information that had to have been devastating.

Parker placed his hand on hers. "It doesn't make it right how he spoke to you. It's my life. He's not my parent, and even if he was, I'm an adult. It's all so fucked up," he muttered.

Emily managed a smile despite the lingering hurt along with the fact that, despite his reasons, Ethan's words had hit home.

"There's one more reason he came to the conclusion he did." Parker drew a deep breath and Emily sensed whatever he was about to say held more sway than Ethan's own personal issues.

"I'm listening."

He glanced down at their intertwined hands. "I told you that Rina died. What I didn't tell you was that, not long after, her parents came to me asking for money. They listed all these things they needed the funds for and I was so wrapped up in grief and guilt for living when she didn't, I paid them."

Emily narrowed her gaze. "Okay?" She knew something was missing in the story, a connection that would make her understand more.

"It became excessive. Year after year. I tried to say no but they'd cry about how much they missed their daughter, about all the things she'd never be able to do and the debt they'd accrued. Medical bills, her student loans."

He didn't look at her then and she remained silent, giving him the time to tell the story in his own way. She wasn't sure what to feel about these people who'd suffered the ultimate loss, but she felt for Parker, who felt so guilty.

He stared at the flowered comforter on her bed and finally spoke again. "Right before I came on this trip, Ethan found out and did some digging. Turns out they were using the money to fund a complete life of luxury on my dime. He told me they were playing on guilt I had no business feeling. It wasn't like I caused the car accident that killed their daughter." He swallowed hard. "I was furious with him for looking into my life – and told him to mind his own fucking business. Clearly the man doesn't listen."

Emily smiled. "Because he loves you and worries about you. The way he expresses it is the issue." She grew more serious. "But he's right, you know. You don't owe them. They're taking advantage of your grief and guilt." She placed a hand on his shoulder and he covered it with his own.

"I do understand that now. Time away, here with you, has done wonders for my outlook on life. But I can tell you for certain what I'm doing for you and your father? It's not the same thing. I'm finding things that I enjoy here. I'm finding myself again."

She tipped her head to the side. "I'm glad I can give you that. And I'm grateful for all you've done for us. But ... though your brother's way of expressing himself leaves something to be desired, I can understand why he's wary of me. And why he thinks I'm using you for your money."

He whipped his head around to face her. "You didn't know I had money. And after you did, you hid the fact that you tried to get a loan. Don't let Ethan's attitude rub off on you."

She frowned, knowing it wouldn't be easy to get those comments out of her head. "I'll try," she promised for Parker's sake. "But you can't be mad at your brother for wanting what's best for you."

Even if he didn't think she was it.

Not that it mattered. His life, his family, everything was back in New York. If he stayed here much longer, it would only be harder to say goodbye.

"Parker," she said softly. "I think it's time for you

to go home with your brother." She wasn't sure what he was doing here any longer anyway.

The inn renovations were well underway, her father in charge and handling it way more than she ever thought he could. Emily and Harper could deal with their own business, and he could approve plans long distance. All something she thought Ethan, when he got over his accusations, would point out as well.

Parker placed a hand under her chin and tipped her head to face him. "I'm not ready."

"We'll never be ready," she said, throwing herself in there, too, because it was true. She didn't want him to leave but that didn't mean it wasn't the right time.

She found herself under him, his lips hard on hers.

"Isn't your brother downstairs?" she managed to ask.

"I told him to leave. I'm hoping he listened. Either way, I don't much care."

She wasn't about to argue, knowing that this might be her last time with him. She sealed her lips over his, sliding her fingers through his hair and holding him against her. Fast and frenzied, his hips ground against hers, his thick cock arousing her beyond belief.

"Clothes," he muttered, rolling off her. He yanked his sweater over his head, then stood to pull off his jeans and the rest of his clothing.

She loved looking at his bare chest, the muscles

from working out and the light sprinkling of hair there. Tearing her gaze away, she eased her own shirt up and off, unhooked her bra, and shimmied out of the straps, tossing the garment onto the floor. Her leggings came next, and she hooked her fingers into her panties, stripping everything off with them. She glanced up to find him tossing his socks onto the floor at the same time she was pulling off her own.

She grinned as he came back down on top of her, his big, hard body covering hers. Closing her eyes, she let herself soak up everything that was Parker. His masculine scent, the feel of his skin, the heat of his body, all things that she might never get to experience again.

He rocked his hips against her, the heat and hardness of his erection pressing intimately against her, and she moaned, her body surprisingly close to an orgasm.

He levered himself up and poised his erection at her entrance. She anticipated him taking her hard and fast, not the slow way he entered her, ensuring she felt the long, luxurious stroke, and that's how he continued. Touching her with his hands, caressing her skin as he made slow, passionate love to her, shocking her.

Rocking her to her core.

She wished he'd rush, take her out of her head, not give her time to think through how good he felt, how he owned her body, how she'd never love anyone like this again. But apparently he wanted to torture them both, because he did all those things with his warm blue gaze locked on hers. Forcing her to face him and take in his beloved features.

She could feel it with every rocking motion of his hips and the sad look in his eyes.

This was goodbye.

✧   ✧   ✧

LEAVING EMILY IN bed, since she didn't want to experience Ethan again and he didn't blame her, Parker headed downstairs, refusing to think about what had transpired between them. He'd have plenty of time for that when he was back in New York. He'd heard her words loud and clear, and though neither of them wanted him to leave, she was right. He was prolonging the inevitable, making their parting more painful with every precious minute they spent together.

He told himself there was text, phone, and FaceTime. That he could come visit her and vice versa. But it wouldn't be the same. And eventually it would fade. Wasn't that the way of things?

His heart slammed in his chest at the possibility of losing her for good. He didn't want to go, but other than the woman he loved and a piece of commercial property he didn't need to be here to own, what did he have here?

No job, no way to make a living, and he wasn't the type to do nothing for the rest of his life. He might not love his job with Knight Time Industries, but at least he had a place to park his ass every day and a way to make money. He didn't need the income but he sure as hell had pride and he would earn what he lived on.

He walked through the downstairs hall to the kitchen.

Although Parker had told his brother to leave, he had a hunch the bastard would be waiting for him. And sure enough, not only was Ethan still in the kitchen, he was talking to James, laughing at something the man said.

Narrowing his gaze, Parker stepped into the room. "Well, someone's suddenly in a good mood."

"I wouldn't go that far," Ethan said. "But James has a decent sense of humor." He paused. "Also he was telling me his plans for this place and how he wants to fulfill his wife's legacy."

A glance at James and Parker looked back to Ethan. "And suddenly you believe in true love and you're on board?"

Ignoring his snarky comment, Ethan went on. "Then he told me Emily's plans for expanding the coffee shop her friend owns."

Parker remained silent because Ethan didn't deserve more.

"He also expounded on how grateful he is and how he and Emily insisted on formal legal contracts and agreements to pay you back."

James remained silent, letting the brothers hash things out.

Still not satisfied because he didn't owe Ethan an explanation for who he gave money to or under what circumstances, he folded his arms across his chest as if to say, *And?*

"And I jumped to conclusions," he said, an apologetic, wry expression settling on his lips, which was something, coming from Ethan. "Can we speak privately?"

It wasn't enough. He'd ripped into Emily without even knowing her.

"I'll apologize to her," Ethan added, his tone sincere, as he pretty much read Parker's mind.

And dammit, this was why it was hard to stay mad at his brother. "Fine. Let's take this into the family room. James, do you mind?"

"Have at it, boys." Parker sensed he wouldn't be so nice if he knew how Ethan had spoken to his daughter.

Ethan followed him into the big room and sat down on the chair, leaving the sofa for his brother. "I fucked up," Ethan said, both hands in the air. "Plain and simple. They seem like a good, solid family."

"They are."

"And my own situation may have colored my judgment."

Parker cocked an eyebrow. "May have?"

"Did."

"You can't stay this angry. It isn't healthy."

Ethan pushed himself to a standing position and began to pace. "Yeah, well, you tell yourself that after your wife fucks a drug dealer and steals from your company to fund her habit."

Parker winced, glancing over at James, glad to see the other man had disappeared, probably gone to his room.

"Fine. So here's the deal. I won't tell you how to live your life and you'll stop digging into and telling me how to live mine. Sound fair?"

"Touché." Shoving his hands into his front pants pockets, Ethan turned to face him.

"Good. Now you should know I've decided to come back home with you. It's time."

Ethan cocked his head to one side. "I thought you loved this woman. How do you go from love to leaving in the span of one fuck session upstairs?"

Hands curling into fists, Parker glared at his brother. "I swear to God–"

Ethan chuckled and Parker shot him a dirty look. Then he sobered and went on. "It's going to kill me to leave as it is. As Emily pointed out, the longer I stay, the harder saying goodbye will be."

Ethan sat back down and leaned forward in his seat. "Bring her with you," he said as if it were simple.

"I wish, but her roots are as deep here as the trees out there. Her father, her best friend, this inn, her new business. She loves all those things. I wouldn't ask her to give them up for me."

Ethan studied him. "Then for the first time in my life, I have no advice to give."

Smiling wryly, Parker agreed with his brother's assessment. "Me, neither. So I'm going to do the sensible thing and head home and figure out what I'm doing with my life." The painful thing. The thing that was like ripping his heart from his chest. "We both know my life is in Manhattan. My family, my business ... what would I do with myself out here? I'm sure as hell not going to teach skiing even if I did get back on the slopes," he said. "And I can't fathom not working for a living."

Ethan groaned. "I'm sorry, man."

"Me, too." He took in his brother's overall look for the first time and laughed. "I see you haven't gotten a haircut."

Ethan raised his finger in an *F-you* gesture.

202

This conversation finished, Parker went upstairs to pack and say goodbye.

✦   ✦   ✦

EMILY STOOD IN the family room with Parker and Ethan. Her father had been shocked to discover Parker was leaving, but they'd said their goodbyes and profuse thank yous on both sides, James for all Parker had done since he'd arrived and Parker for her father's hospitality.

A lump lodged in her throat and she was in a state of internal panic. Why had she told him to go home? They could have had more time … but she knew it would have been a mistake. More time to get used to him being in the house, to sleeping in his bed, to having him help her with her deliveries to town in the morning or sharing coffee together before they drove in.

He had to be getting bored with nothing to do but take walks, drive to town, or hang around the inn. No, she thought sadly, she'd done the right thing for them both.

And he knew it, too, or he'd never have agreed to go.

"Emily, I was hoping we could start over," Ethan said, distracting her from her painful reality.

She glanced at the imposing man who had all but

verbally ripped her to shreds earlier and had to remind herself he was Parker's brother. He'd been his pseudo-parent and Parker loved him.

She assumed Parker had had a talk with Ethan earlier, and for Parker's sake, she nodded. "Sure. That would be good."

"I'm sorry. I was…" Ethan trailed off and Parker slammed him in the rib with his elbow.

"An utter and complete ass and I'm sorry," Ethan said, coughing over his brother's unsubtle and probably too hard jab.

"Thank you. I accept your apology. But for the future, you might want to work on your people skills," she said, unable to hold back some of her feelings.

Beside her, Parker chuckled, and to her surprise, Ethan let out a loud laugh.

"Feisty. I can see the attraction and why you love her." He paused. "I'll go out to the car. Give you two a few minutes alone," Ethan said.

He headed out to his rental car and Parker turned to face her.

"You're going to kill me but I'm hiring a private investigator to look into Rex. I want to find something on the bastard that I can take to him and use to convince him to give you the divorce. And I'm getting someone to keep an eye on this place until we know you're comfortable and feel safe from him and his uninvited appearances."

Her eyes opened wide at his words. "You're in-sane."

He shook his head. "Don't fight with me. It won't help and you don't want our goodbye to turn into an argument." His grin said he knew he'd won this round.

She drew a deep breath and let it out, then decided agreement was simpler. "Fine. Thank you for looking out for me."

She really would feel safer knowing there was someone around to make sure Rex didn't get out of control. "But you can't keep someone watching me indefinitely."

He merely cocked an eyebrow and she bit down on her cheek. As agreed, she wouldn't argue.

"Let's see. What else?" he asked. "Your father promised to be careful and not cause you any extra worry about him. No more ladders." He gestured toward the basement, where James had taken his fall.

She should have known Parker would leave no stone unturned in taking care of her despite the abruptness of his departure.

She slid her tongue over her dry lips, then said, "I'm having Harper write the checks to our landlord." She half hiccupped, half laughed, which was all in an attempt to hold back a cry. She didn't even want to write out his name, taunting her with what they couldn't have.

Don't cry. Don't cry. Don't cry. She repeated the mantra to herself over and over, not wanting to break down until he was gone. She didn't want his last memory of her to be red eyes and a snotty nose.

He cupped her face in his hand and stared into her eyes. "This is the hardest fucking thing I've ever done and that's saying something," he said in a gruff voice, and she lost the battle, the tears she'd been holding back releasing, trickling down her cheeks.

"I'm going to miss you, city boy," she whispered.

He treated her to a sad smile. "I want to say there's text and phone and FaceTime–"

She shook her head. "I can't be your friend, Parker. Because one day you'll move on and it will break my heart." Her throat burned holding back the bawling cry she wanted to have. "A clean break is much easier." Easier was definitely the wrong word, but knowing he was moving on without her would kill her. She'd rather not know for sure.

He leaned down and pressed his mouth hard against hers, not deepening the kiss, just connecting their lips one last time. "Close your eyes," he whispered against her mouth.

She did.

Then she felt the loss of his touch. His warmth. His presence. She heard the sound of the door closing softly behind him and only then did she fall to the floor and let the real hysterical tears fall.

✧   ✧   ✧

EMILY DIDN'T KNOW how much time had passed when her father came to her side and helped her to her feet. It could have been five minutes or an hour. She had no idea, she just knew the sobs racking her body were real and endless and her throat felt raw.

Her dad sat with her on the sofa and let her cry it out until she was ready to pull herself together. "Thanks, Dad. I'm so lucky to have you." She hugged him tight, his familiar scent giving her a sense of peace despite her pain.

"Honey, I'm fifty-eight going on fifty-nine. I'm not ancient. You have to stop seeing me the way your mother was when she was sick and dying, and start viewing me the way I really am. Now let's focus on you. You love that man and you let him go?"

She pulled herself back and met his gaze. "His job and family are in New York."

"Did you consider going with him?"

She blinked in surprise. "My life is here. You're here. I have a business to put into motion … and he didn't ask me." Her heart pounded in her chest. "But he knows how much I love it here. This town, you, Harper, you're all part of who I am. I couldn't leave and go back to a city." She shook her head. "He knows me too well to ask."

Her father frowned. "You young people—"

"*Now* you sound old." She let out a laugh.

"I just mean that you young people don't realize how important love is until sometimes it's too late. I saw how you two looked at each other…"

"It's done, Dad. Let's not talk about it anymore, okay? I'll take a day or two and then I'll pull myself together. We have wallpaper to pick, carpet to choose, and a whole kitchen to design. Not to mention Harper and I are meeting with an architect on Monday." But despite listing all she had to look forward to, the pain in the center of her chest remained.

Chapter Ten

A WEEK AFTER Parker's departure, Emily was still miserable, but Harper, to her credit, ignored Emily's moods, which made it easier to push forward. She immersed herself in work and she had plenty of it to keep her busy.

After a particularly trying day of arguing with places on how long the furniture she wanted for the rooms for the inn would take, she turned in to bed early. She and Harper were on hold until the architect finished the plans and they were approved. Then there would be the construction phase, so for now it was business as usual at Harper's Coffee Shop soon to be Harper and Em's Bake and Brew.

She was just about to fall asleep when the sound of the doorbell ringing startled her. She pulled on her sweats and shirt and headed downstairs. She was much more careful now about opening the door, even keeping it locked during the day, and she glanced through the peephole.

True to his word, Parker had hired a bodyguard

firm and there was a day and night shift keeping an eye on Emily. She'd never really thought she would need it. Except as she looked out now, she saw the man who'd introduced himself as Dave, or night-shift guy, as she mentally called him, stood holding on to Rex by the collar as he rang the doorbell again.

Her stomach flipped as she opened the door. "Umm, hi?" she said at the same time Rex began to yell.

"Emily, tell this goon I'm your husband and to let me in!"

"Ma'am?" Dave, with his shaved head, broad shoulders, and big body, asked. "Is he your husband? He looks like the photograph we were given of the man to look out for. And I caught him sneaking around the house as if casing it. And when I met up with him by his car, I smelled gasoline. I think there are cans in the trunk."

Emily blinked. "No, he's not my husband, he's my soon-to-be ex-husband." And he was dressed all in black. Camouflage at night.

"Dammit, Emily, there's no distinction. I love you. When are you going to come to your senses and come home with me?"

She folded her arms across her chest. A glance at the empty staircase told her her dad was still upstairs. Thank God for Ambien. "Are there gas cans in the trunk? Is that what he smells?" she asked Rex.

He looked away guiltily.

"Should I call the police?" her bodyguard asked.

"Yes, please."

Dave immediately pulled out his cell phone and dialed 911, talking while Rex, whose eyes opened wide in horror, started to scream. "What? Emily, no. Don't, please. I was just trying to convince you to come back to Chicago with me."

"How? By burning down my house?" she said just as loudly.

"I thought if the inn burned, you'd have no choice but to turn back to me. I'd have helped your father rebuild. You'd be grateful to me and we could be together," he said.

She knew he was insane. When she looked back, she'd been able to see the signs of narcissism and a Svengali complex, trying to mold her into his perfect woman. But she'd never pegged him as truly dangerous, having convinced herself the fall down the stairs was an accident. Now she wasn't so sure. If she'd had the baby, he wouldn't have had her all to himself.

The police finally arrived and cuffed a hysterical Rex. The noxious smell of gas gave them probable cause to search his vehicle for dangerous substances, and they found three full cans of gasoline. In the front of the car was a pile of lighters.

Thank God Parker had thought ahead to hire a bodyguard, and as soon as she thought of him, tears filled her eyes once more. Dammit. She was going to get through a day without crying. One day. Soon.

✧   ✧   ✧

PARKER STOOD IN Ethan's office, looking out the window at the Upper East Side of Manhattan. The sun was shining, people down below looked like tiny specks, ants rushing around to one place or another.

Ethan sat at his desk, tapping his favorite pen against a blotter.

Sebastian and his wife, Ashley, sat side-by-side on one corner of the leather sofa, cuddling like the lovebirds they were. Sierra and her husband, Ryder, did the same on the other side.

All eyes were on Parker, waiting for him to speak since he'd called this family meeting. The minute he had stepped foot on the private plane Ethan had chartered to go to Denver, Parker knew he'd made a mistake. Hell, he'd known as he kissed Emily goodbye, her salty tears mixed with her innate sweetness, that walking away was the wrong, worst thing he could do.

But the plane took off and soon he'd been in the air, alone with his thoughts for a solid five-plus hours. And during that time, he'd come to some pretty heavy conclusions.

"Is someone going to tell us why we're here?" Sebastian asked.

"Patience, young grasshopper," Ashley said and chuckled. Apparently they'd been watching old movies.

"I needed to talk to everyone. I have news."

Ethan didn't know for sure what Parker was going to say, but of everyone here, he'd seen Parker firsthand after leaving Emily behind. He had to know what was coming. But he sat behind his desk, his expression giving nothing away.

"Parker met a girl in Colorado," Sebastian announced.

"What am I? A lovesick teenager? I met a woman there. And her father. And I got involved in their business…" He shook his head, trying to get back on track. "I fell in love," he finally said, summing up the only thing that mattered.

"And then the dumb ass left her behind." This from Ethan, who finally opened his mouth. He was still an asshole. His dealings with Emily hadn't taught him anything at all.

Everyone whispered amongst themselves. Or rather the two couples whispered. Ethan sat in silence.

"I'm going back."

"Another vacation? To see her?" Ashley asked, sounding pleased for him.

"Umm, no. I'm moving to Colorado. For good." His words came with the force of a bomb dropping. Shocked silence followed.

At first no one said a word.

And then the questions overlapped each other. Parker whistled to shut them all up. "Here's the deal." He figured he was covering everyone's questions. "The main thing holding me back all along was, what would I do there? I can't sit around and I need to make a living. I refuse to live off of family money or money from this business if I'm not working it."

Ethan looked at him in admiration, Sebastian in shock but a slow grin was spreading across his face. His younger brother was into romance these days, so he would support Parker one hundred percent. Ethan might not like the distance between them, but having seen Parker's reaction to Ethan verbally hurting Emily, he knew where Parker's heart lay. Ethan's own heart might be broken and in shambles, but he still loved his siblings and wanted them to be happy.

"I'm happy for you," Sebastian said.

"Me, too." Sierra jumped up and gave him a hug. "But I'm going to miss you so much."

Parker chuckled. "Same, sis, but you'll come visit and we'll come here."

"When do we get to meet her?" Ashley asked.

"Well, Ethan already did and made one hell of an

impression." Parker's voice darkened at the memory.

"Oh, Ethan," Sierra said. "What did you do?" She wagged her finger at him.

"It was ugly," Ethan admitted. "But we parted on good terms."

Parker doubted she'd forgotten how Ethan had spoken to her. Mending that relationship would take time. "Listen, I plan on going back there to convince her to marry me." He patted the ring he'd personally chosen that now sat securely in his pocket.

Ashley and Sierra squealed their excitement and Parker grinned.

"Then I'll bring her home to meet all of you. She's already dealt with the scary one." He jerked a finger over his shoulder to Ethan. "The rest of you are a piece of cake." He grinned. "Speaking of cake, Emily is a baker."

"Oh, yum. That's going to be fun at family gatherings," Ashley said and Parker chuckled.

He just hoped Emily hadn't given up on him. It had only been a week, but he'd left her. Her biggest fear had been losing those she loved and he'd put her in that very position.

"Parker, you didn't say what you're going to be doing out there workwise," Sebastian said, interrupting his train of thought.

"Aah." He leaned against Ethan's desk. "While I

was there, I ran into a guy I knew from my skiing days. Caleb Benson. He owns a ski shop that's also a sports retail store. He's looking to expand into other areas of Colorado, to start. But he didn't have the capital or someone to run it with. I gave him a call. I'm going to work with him, see if I like it, and if so, we're going into partnership."

"Awesome. That's right up your alley!" Sebastian rose and walked over, slapping him on the back. "Good for you. You never belonged here behind a desk." He paused, then said, "Can I ask you a question?"

"Go for it."

"Did you ski again while you were out there?"

Parker shook his head, but he'd come to realize how ridiculous those fears of getting back on the slopes really were. "I think I associated the skiing with Rina, the car accident and her death. Since I've been back in New York, missing Colorado and Emily, I took care of some loose ends from those days."

He'd visited the Londons and told Elana and George that their emotional blackmail was over. They'd been upset but they also realized they'd taken advantage of Parker and there was nothing they could hold over him to get him to pay. He was free of the past, only his good memories of Rina remaining.

Ethan nodded approvingly. "Good for you, Parker. It's about time."

Parker actually agreed with his sibling. He also believed they'd come to an understanding about staying out of each other's personal lives or choices unless asked or invited in.

That didn't mean the others shouldn't look over their shoulders, he thought wryly.

"So that's my news," Parker said. "And I wanted to share it with the people I love. And the ones I'm going to miss. So you'd all better plan on visiting us in Colorado."

He only hoped there would be an *us* when he arrived.

EMILY WAS ARM deep in flour, baking bread. Not angry baking. Not hurt baking. Just very emotional baking because she needed the release. She wore her *Kiss the Cook* apron, had her hair pulled into a floppy, messy ponytail, nixed the makeup because she wasn't leaving the house and she didn't wear much on a regular day anyway, and flipped on music.

Because she was feeling sentimental, she picked Queen, the same album she and Parker had listened to on their way to the resort, where they'd shared an amazing couple of days. Not letting her mind wander *there*, she focused on the music and found herself singing to "Crazy Little Thing Called Love."

Just wonderful, she thought to herself. Then again what had she expected when she'd chosen these songs? She kneaded the bread, then rolled the dough with the ceramic rolling pin, her mind never wandering much past Parker.

It had been two weeks since she'd seen him. Two weeks since she'd heard his voice. Felt his strong arms around her. Nope, she wasn't over him yet. Not by a long shot. But she didn't regret telling him not to keep in touch. Without a doubt, she knew she couldn't handle idle chitchat about their lives without falling apart and begging him to come back. And let's face it. If he wanted to be here badly enough, he'd have found a way to make it work.

Just like she could have asked to join him in New York?

She pinched the bridge of her nose, wondering not for the first time if she'd made the ultimate mistake not broaching the subject. Of letting herself consider moving to Manhattan to be with the man she loved.

Her dad would always be her dad. Her sister lived in Florida and they were all still close. As for Harper? Her best friend in the entire world would understand. Emily just hadn't been brave enough to even let herself consider the idea, and now she was knee deep in architectural plans and she owed Parker money that she could only pay back by building the property and making the shop a success.

God, what a mess she'd made of her life.

She was alone here for the afternoon. Her father was at lunch with Dr. Carlysle in town. As for the inn's future, they had plans in place. Emily had chosen the wallpaper, carpet, and furniture through an online site that offered decoration help and they should be up and running within a few months.

Once they were ready, they'd place an ad with the local paper in their print edition they left at all businesses and their online site for housekeeping and cooking help. They anticipated the renovations to continue through the summer, then a slow fall season with more of a soft opening until they could get a website up and running and word out about their accommodations.

As for Emily and Harper, the architect brought them plans they'd loved and approved. With the town being small, permits should be approved quickly and construction should start soon. Harper would be able to keep the coffee shop open for a good part of the work. Meanwhile they were doing research on what they wanted for décor. It was exciting. Invigorating. Or should be, if she could share it with Parker.

She blew out a deep breath and began to cut the dough into the right size when the front door opened.

"Hello?" she called out.

Now that Rex had been arrested and because he was considered dangerous, not given bail, she was comfortable going back to the unlocked, visitors-welcome policy they'd had before.

Nobody answered, so she wiped her hands on her apron and started for the entryway, stopping short when she laid eyes on Parker. She let out a startled gasp, then blinked a few times to make sure she wasn't dreaming or conjuring him up because she wanted it to be him so badly.

"Parker?" He'd trimmed his scruffy beard, keeping the overall effect that he'd achieved while not shaving during his time in Colorado, and he wore a navy Henley and a pair of jeans, and the red light down jacket he'd bought at Caleb Benson's.

"In the flesh."

She tipped her head to the side, her heart pounding hard in her chest. "Why?" she asked, that damned lump that was always in her throat still there, only bigger.

"Because I missed you." His blue eyes sparkled with mirth and happiness.

They still stood feet apart but she needed to know more before getting her hopes up. "So you came for a visit?"

"Actually I packed up my car and drove across the

damned country. I'm back for good." He shook his head. "I'm back for you. Forever."

She finally let herself believe.

Breathe.

With a squeal, she ran for him, jumping into his arms and peppering kisses all over his face. "Oh my God, I missed you. I didn't know how I was going to get through losing you. I was contemplating moving to New York, but I was so entrenched here with the coffee shop and renovations–"

"Emily?"

"Yes?"

"Shut up and kiss me," he said with a grin.

And then her lips were on his, her tongue in his mouth, and all was right in her world. He kissed her until she was dizzy and gasping for air. It was only when she lifted her head and looked into his eyes that she realized something important.

"I never told you," she said.

That blue gaze held on to hers. "I know."

She pressed her hands against his cheeks and said, "I love you, Parker Knight. And I never want to be without you again."

Something akin to relief crossed his face as he slid her down his body. He reached into his pocket, then to her utter shock, he lowered himself to one knee.

"Emily Ann Stevens, will you spend the rest of our

lives making me the happiest man alive? Will you marry me?"

She gasped as he revealed a very large ring by her small-town standards, but a tasteful and gorgeous ring with a round stone and two rubies on either side.

"The rubies are for your mom. So you'll always know she's with you."

She blinked, forcing the tears that had been welling in her eyes to fall. "I can't believe you thought about that. I love it."

"Well?" he asked. "Before my bad knee gives out?"

"Yes!" she squealed, pulling him to a standing position before wrapping her arms around his neck and kissing him hard.

"Did she say yes yet?" Her father's voice sounded from outside.

Laughing, Parker pulled her against him as they turned to face the front door. "Come in, James. Harper."

She and Harper hugged, squealed, and did the girl thing. Then she turned to her dad. "You knew?"

"I wasn't going to ask you to marry me without your father's permission," Parker said, pressing a kiss to the top of her head.

"I can't say it was easy to keep a secret, either, not with you moping around here," James said with a huge grin.

Emily turned to Harper. "You knew?" she asked in shock.

"Oh hell no," Parker muttered. "I called her on my way here. I didn't trust her not to give away the surprise."

Harper pouted but she was laughing.

And Emily had everyone who mattered with her at the most important moment in her life. Best of all, she had the man of her dreams.

"What are you going to do here?" she asked.

He swiped at her nose. "Flour," he said with a grin. "I have plans, baby. Big plans."

"As long as they include me, I'm happy."

And she was. Unbelievably, incredibly happy and she never intended to take one day with Parker for granted.

Epilogue

PARKER PACKED AWAY his skis in the garage of the house he'd built on land he and Emily had purchased not long after he'd moved to Colorado. They weren't comfortable living with her father and Parker wanted a place of their own. The house wasn't far from the inn where James lived and ran his bed-and-breakfast, making Emily happy.

After settling in, he'd wanted to make things legal with Emily quickly and had flown his entire family out to join them for the wedding. Emily loved his siblings and their spouses ... well, everyone but Ethan, who she still watched warily but tried to win over with her delicious baked goods.

Parker knew that once Ethan moved on from what had happened with Mandy and returned to being the man he once was, he and Emily would get along fine. She said she wasn't giving up on him despite his surly disposition. Her words, and they fit.

At the urging of both Emily and Caleb, his new partner, he'd begun to ski again, for fun. To his surprise, he found he missed it more than he'd realized or let himself acknowledge. It was a big part of him at one time and he'd cut himself off from it completely. He was grateful to have it back, and he couldn't help but feel he had Emily to thank for opening his heart again. To so many things.

He walked into the rustic home and immediately inhaled the familiar scent of Snickerdoodles, the cookie she'd begun to bake for him every time he went out to ski. He'd come home and she'd greet him with cookies, sipping her hot chocolate as he devoured half the plate at one sitting.

She and Harper had opened their business and it was a huge success. They'd hired a cake baker, which enabled them to cater parties as well. They had a good, reliable staff and things were going well for them. He was extremely proud of her.

She stood in the kitchen, rinsing off the mixer beaters. He loved watching her do the basic things she loved, knowing she got pleasure out of baking and making their house a home while running a business she loved.

"Hey, gorgeous," he said, immediately reaching for the cookies waiting for him on a plate.

Catching sight of him, she wiped her hands on a towel and walked over, giving him a kiss.

"Hey, yourself." She smiled. "I'm glad you're

home. There's something I've been dying to tell you."

He raised his eyebrows. "What's that?"

Grasping his hand, she pulled him out of the kitchen, a state-of-the-art room he'd given her as a gift, and led him to the bedroom.

"Sit," she said, bracing her hands on his shoulders and lowering him to the mattress on the bed.

"Now close your eyes."

Last time he'd told her to close her eyes, he'd left. But trusting her, he warily shut his lids.

He heard footsteps, then she said, "Open." In her hand, she held out a pregnancy test with two distinct pink lines. "Congratulations, Daddy."

"Holy shit." Seriously holy shit. They knew they wanted kids but they hadn't discussed how soon.

"Remember that bout of strep throat? Apparently antibiotics lessen the pill's effectiveness. We weren't thinking about that when we…"

Laughing, he rose and tossed her gently onto the bed, coming down on top of her. "I didn't think you could make me any happier but you just did."

Her wide smile told him she was relieved at his re-action. "I wasn't that worried but … you never know."

He kissed her forehead, her nose, her lips. "Now you know for sure." And then he went on to make love to his wife.

The soon-to-be mother of his child.

Life truly couldn't get any better.

Thanks for reading!

Next up is Ethan Knight and Sienna Dare's story in DARE ME TONIGHT.

Also

Don't miss Harper Sanders and Matt Banks short story in TAKE ME NOW.

Keep reading for a DARE ME TONIGHT sneak peek!

DARE ME TONIGHT EXCERPT

S IENNA DARE WALKED into her half brother Ian's office in the Miami Thunder Stadium, still in awe of the fact that she had any kind of relationship with Ian at all, given their crazy dynamic. It had taken him years to accept her part of the family in his life, considering Sienna's mom had been their father's mistress. In true soap opera tradition, Robert Dare had two families. But they'd been working on making their peace as adults, and here they were now.

Considering how much she needed Ian's advice on her future, Sienna was grateful. She'd normally ask her older brothers for help, but Alex was away with his wife, Madison, on a business trip, and Jason was in New York City, running his nightclubs.

Her parents? Her father hadn't been around much lately, and her mother seemed wrapped up in whatever drama followed her father now. Sienna refused to think much about her parents' personal lives. She had enough to worry about on her own.

She knocked on the door, and knowing Ian was expecting her, she stepped inside.

"What the hell did you do to your hair?"

She'd barely had a foot in the door when Ian raised his voice. And to think, she'd wondered if he'd even notice the change.

"Don't you like it?" She pulled on the long pony-tail, grinning at the dark strands she saw in her peripheral vision.

Ian scowled. "You were blonde last time I saw you."

"And now I'm not. I dyed it." She sat down on the couch across the room from his desk, not put off by his typical bluster.

Maybe when she'd first met Ian, he'd frightened her with his gruff exterior, but she'd seen him with his sisters – his full-blooded sisters, Olivia and Avery – and knew there was a heart beneath the brusqueness. And lately, he'd extended that... she wouldn't call it sweetness... more like caring to her, as well. It helped that Alex worked for Ian at the Thunder team. The family was coming together. Considering *she* was the reason they'd been torn apart, the rapprochement made Sienna happy.

Ian was still frowning at her dark hair.

"Well, I like it," she informed him. "It's part of me finding myself," she said, not willing to be steamrolled.

He pushed himself to a standing position, looking imposing as ever in his suit and tie, and walked over joining her on the couch. "Look, I understand you graduated college and you're confused about what to do with your life."

She swallowed hard. "You can say that again. I'm twenty-three years old. I lost a year of school when I was sick, so I'm really old enough that I ought to know what I want. But I don't."

He tapped a pen on the table in front of him. "You have good choices ahead of you though. You're an extremely bright woman. You graduated summa cum laude in management and business, and you have an offer for a full scholarship to attend Columbia's exclusive Digital Business Strategy program. And I happen to know you've received an invitation to attend their NYC Weekend Scholars' Social starting this Saturday."

She raised an eyebrow at her half brother. "I can

see why Avery says you know all and see all." She'd been avoiding RSVP'ing to the weekend event and she'd let the due date to reply lapse because she'd known then she'd have to make a decision on the program.

He shrugged. "I make it my business to know about my family and those I care about." He lowered his voice as he said, "You've become one of those people, Sienna."

She shifted uncomfortably. "Because I was the sick one? The baby with childhood leukemia?" She'd been in remission since she was seven thanks to the generosity of Avery's bone marrow donation.

Her dad, Robert Dare, had gone to his legitimate family, told them about his mistress and family on the side, blown their worlds and his marriage sky-high, and asked the kids to be tested to save Sienna. Her mother had known about the other wife and family all along. The kids had learned when the fallout happened. Not so for Ian and his side of the family.

"No, not because you were once sick," Ian said with a definitive shake of his head. "Because you're you and you've been nothing but good and kind to my siblings. And to me even when I was a jerk." His lips twitched, as much of a smile as Ian Dare gave. "So about the weekend in New York. I think you should go. It will give you good perspective on what to expect from the school and an idea about whether you'd like living in Manhattan."

She pulled her bottom lip between her teeth. "I, umm, let the RSVP lapse."

He rolled his broad shoulders, dismissing her concern. "And I took care of that for you. I told the school you'd be coming and I did you one better. I called an acquaintance of mine who is going to be your escort for the weekend."

"Ian!" He was so presumptuous and pushy. But wasn't that why she was here? So he'd help her make decisions?

"The school would have assigned you to someone anyway. This way you get someone I trust. Ethan Knight's company gives major donations to the school and to this program in particular," he went on, ignoring her outburst. "He'll take you to the formal the first night and give you an upscale tour of Manhattan the next day. By the time you leave, you'll have a good idea of whether the program is right for you. No pressure. And I know you'll be in good hands," he said, sounding very pleased with himself.

She sighed. She'd grown used to Ian's dominating personality. All the Dare siblings had, legitimate and illegitimate alike. "Fine. But can I get a flight to New York this late in the week?" Today was Thursday. She'd have to be there on Saturday.

"The corporate jet is fueled and ready for you. Any other concerns?" Ian asked.

A broad smile pulled at her lips. Now that he'd laid it out for her so simply, the weekend seemed more like an adventure than a chore or something that would make her feel coerced.

"I suppose I ought to go pack!" She bounced up from her seat, suddenly eager to check out Manhattan and experience this weekend, starting with the private jet. Her father, the hotel magnate, didn't fly them that way despite his wealth.

Sienna was all about new experiences. She supposed it had to do with nearly losing her life at such a young age. Although making permanent decisions about her future felt overwhelming, the easy things, like changing her hair, which she knew what it was like to lose, or going to check out New York City by herself, were exciting.

And she was looking forward to meeting the donor who would be her escort for the weekend.

✧   ✧   ✧

ETHAN KNIGHT NEEDED a break. Hell, after the year he'd had, he deserved one. But as luck would have it lately, shit was piling up in every way.

His billion-dollar project for the Miami Thunder Football Stadium was a pain in the ass. The schematics for the deliverables had changed several times, and if a situation could go wrong, it did. His company, Knigh Time Technology, KTT for short, supplied high-tech security for smart buildings and state-of-the-ar corporate parks, and now, thanks to Ian Dare, a brand-new stadium. If they nailed this project, many more sports complexes and technology projects could come their way.

Needless to say, keeping Ian Dare happy had become a full-time job. The man was as hands-on as Ethan. Two demanding CEOs and Ethan had to do his best to accommodate the other man, not butt heads with him.

"What's up?" Sebastian, Ethan's brother, who also worked for KTT, asked.

"You wouldn't believe it if I told you." Ethan strode to the window in his office overlooking Manhattan and groaned.

"Try me," his youngest brother said.

Ethan shrugged. "Ian Dare's youngest sister is coming to New York this weekend. You know the Weekend Scholars' Social that Columbia hosts and we send a representative to in order to induce the brightest to attend their business school?"

"So we can hire them after? Sure do. I used to be the guy who attended on the company's behalf remember? I was more than happy to turn that job over to people on our management team."

Sebastian shuddered at the memory, which didn't do much to make Ethan feel better about the upcoming event.

"Ian wants me to escort her personally," Ethan said.

Sebastian burst out laughing. "Oh, that's rich. Mr. Antisocial is going to make small talk with a graduate student-to-be."

Ethan turned around and faced Sebastian, leaning against the window, annoyed by his brother's obvious amusement at Ethan's expense. "She's twenty-three, almost twenty-four according to Ian. Not that much of a child." Just enough to get on his nerves with chatter, compared to his ripe old age of thirty-one. Lord knew, after all he'd been through, he felt ancient.

Still smirking, Sebastian said, "Maybe it'll be good for you. You know, get you out of the apartment and mingling with actual human beings. People who aren't family or minions that you can't yell at all the time?"

"Wiseass." Ethan ran a hand through his overly long hair.

"Well, the Thunder Stadium is priority one, so make sure you show this woman a good time. Smile a little. Maybe cut your hair?" Sebastian cocked an eyebrow.

Ethan scowled, annoyed. His brothers had been

giving him shit about the length of his hair for a while now. Almost a year, to be precise. He used to be so meticulous, suits and ties pressed just so, hair cut every month by a ridiculously expensive guy at a salon, and he thought he was pleasing his wife.

Well, considering the wife had died of a self-induced accidental drug overdose and had also been undermining and stealing from his company, working with a supplier on a huge project to use substandard material and pocket the difference so she could support her drug habit, Ethan figured it was time for a lot of changes.

He was no longer going to twist himself inside out for a woman who wouldn't appreciate anything he did or gave to her anyway. Been there, done that.

He'd get through this weekend and go back to his happy hermit life.

✧　✧　✧

SIENNA LOVED THE private jet experience, felt like a princess for the two-and-a-half-hour flight, and now she was ready to take on Manhattan. She strode through the airport, looking for a sign with her last name on it. Ian had given her the name of her companion, Ethan Knight, and had assured her the man would be here himself to pick her up.

When she finally caught sight of her last name on a

236

placard, a woman was holding up the card. With a shrug, Sienna headed toward the pretty female with light brown hair and blonde highlights, wearing a summer floral dress and shoes Sienna envied.

As she approached, Sienna waved. "Hi," she said, coming to a stop. "I'm Sienna Dare."

The woman flashed a genuine smile. "Nice to meet you. I'm Sierra Hammond, Ethan's sister. I'm so sorry he couldn't be here himself but there was an emergency at the office." Tucking the sign under her arm, she extended her hand, which Sienna shook.

"Sienna and Sierra. Cute," Sienna said, laughing.

The other woman chuckled. "I noticed the similarities, too."

"Thank you for picking me up."

"My brother really wanted to be here," Sierra said, obviously trying to reassure her.

Sienna waved away the woman's concerns. "I'm fine. Really." Sienna wasn't insulted in the least. If Ethan Knight was anything like Ian, he wouldn't have the time to be on airport duty.

Sierra seemed to relax at Sienna's easy attitude. "Okay, good. Well, I thought I'd take you to the apartment where you'll be staying and show you around. Do you need to wait for luggage?"

"No. I fit everything into my carry on." Sienna smiled brightly. "We're not going to a hotel?"

"No, my family owns a building on the Upper Eas Side of Manhattan. We have an apartment for out-of town guests and Ethan thought you'd be more com fortable there."

"Sounds good."

They chatted on the limousine ride to the apart ment. Sierra sat in the back beside Sienna, the drive knowing where to take them. Sienna discovered tha Sierra was married to her longtime love, Ryder Ham mond, with a baby girl at home. She also ran the Socia Media Division at Knight Time Technology.

Listening to how the twenty-five-year-old womar had her life together made Sienna feel wistful that she wasn't anywhere near doing the same. But that was what this weekend was about, she reminded herself trying not to feel too bad about herself. She had time to figure it all out.

She was led into a gorgeous apartment that was well decorated, with dark wood furniture and a leather sofa in the family room. She rolled her suitcase into the spacious entry area and set it off to the side.

"So this is it," Sierra said. "The bedroom is tha door over there." She pointed to a back corner with a closed door. "The refrigerator is stocked, but anything you need, I want you to feel comfortable calling me."

They exchanged numbers, programming them into their phones.

"There's an itinerary on the table in the family room, but there will be a limo picking you up tonight for the gala, and my brother will be meeting you there. I promise," Sierra reassured her with a smile.

"No worries. It's all good."

Sierra hesitated. "I hate to just leave you, but I need to get home. We just wanted someone from the family to pick you up and make you feel comfortable, but if you need a tour guide for the afternoon…"

With a shake of her head, Sienna calmed the other woman. "I think I'll head over to one of the department stores and have my makeup done for tonight," she said, the idea popping into her head. And since she'd taken an early-morning flight, Sienna had the entire afternoon free. "I'm really used to being on my own. I'm fine."

"Oh, makeup sounds like fun. I wish I could join you. Do you want to get your hair done, too? Have the whole experience? My stylist is a friend. I'm sure he could fit you in?" Sierra offered. "Not that I'm saying you need your hair done." She sounded horrified at her choice of words.

Sienna burst out laughing. She really liked Sierra Hammond. "As a matter of fact, I would love to have my hair done for tonight."

Sierra pulled out her phone and dialed the salon, arranged a time, and ended the call. "All set. I'll text you the information. The car is at your disposal–"

Sienna shook her head. "I can take an Uber or a taxi, honest. It'll be fun to explore the city that way.

"No can do." Sierra shifted her purse higher on her shoulder. "I promised Ethan I'd take good care of you and that means the full chauffeured deal. Enjoy your time in New York," she said, starting for the door.

Before leaving, she turned back around. "Umm … about my brother."

"Yes?"

"He can be…" She drew a breath and paused, as if hesitating about what to say. Finally she settled on a word. "Abrasive on a good day." She winced at her own choice. "I mean–"

"Don't worry. Ian Dare is my half brother. I know how to deal with gruff, uptight men."

"I hope you do," Sierra said before shooting Sienna a hopeful smile and walking out, shutting the door behind her.

✧　✧　✧

SIENNA HAD A fantastic afternoon getting herself made up for the night's event. Not only did she splurge, purchasing a ton of makeup and skin-care products after having her face done up at Saks Fifth Avenue, she left the salon with her newly dyed hair

240

now blow-dried and curled.

She called Jason and talked him into meeting her for coffee because she was in town and when else could she see him? He seemed subdued, which was par for the course with her sibling, his life having taken an unexpected turn back in his college days. One event had changed and marked him forever. But she'd made him smile and she called that a win.

Then she took the limo back to the apartment and headed upstairs with a bounce in her step.

Excited, she decided to call Avery and show her the end results of her day. After dumping all the bags on the bed, she pulled out her phone and Facetimed her half sister, who had, over the years, become one of her closest friends. Maybe all the Dares weren't BFFs, but the girls had definitely bridged the gap their father had created.

After the call rang a few times, Avery's face appeared on the screen. "Hi! How's New York?" she asked.

"Amazing. I pampered myself. Look." Sienna grinned into the camera phone and blew her a kiss, showing off her red lipstick.

"Oh, gorgeous!" Avery, a video blogger and married to one of the biggest rock stars in the world, Grey Kingston, lead guitarist and songwriter for the band Tangled Royal, knew a good makeover when she saw one. "And I really love your hair so dark. It makes your eyes pop!"

Sienna rolled her eyes. "I don't have those violet eyes of yours. Mine are crappy brown."

"Hot chocolate colored," Avery argued. "Now let me see your dress for tonight."

Sienna had hung up the outfit before she'd gone out earlier and she'd brought a travel steamer with her just in case the garment wrinkled. From the closet, she pulled out the little black dress that flared out at the waist and held it up in front of her, showing it off for Avery.

"Ooh, the white piping makes the dress," Avery said, whistling her approval. "Shoes?"

"Mom lent me her black Louboutins." Sienna was more of a down-to-earth girl, but once in a while, dressing up was nice, and her mother's closet was full of fun, luxurious things. She held up the red-soled shoes.

"Nice!" Avery exclaimed.

Sienna and Avery didn't discuss their moms much, that being the one conversation that remained awkward. No matter how she looked at it, Sienna's mom, Savannah, had been Robert Dare's mistress/other woman with another family, while Avery's mom, Emma, had been in the dark. The good news was that Emma had remarried a nice man the family approved of, and that helped everyone get over the past.

"Do you know who you're meeting tonight?" Avery asked.

Sienna placed the dress and shoes on the bed and faced the phone again. "Ethan Knight, CEO of Knight Time Technology. The company is doing the tech and security for Ian's new stadium.

"Have you Googled him?" Avery met her gaze, then disappeared from the screen, leaving it blank, and Sienna knew her sister was already busy on the browser. "Holy shit, he's hot!" she said, her voice coming through the phone.

"Show me. I need to know who to look for tonight."

Avery screenshotted a photo and sent it over Messenger. As soon as Sienna received the picture, she pulled up the photo and sucked in a startled breath.

Sienna had expected a stuffy older man who it would be difficult to spend the weekend with and pay attention to, not a sexy, gorgeous guy. Ethan Knight had dark short hair, with a handsome, freshly shaven face. In his suit and tie, he was the epitome of a CEO in charge of everything and everyone around him.

If not for the fact that she found him hot, she would have said his steely-eyed stare reminded her of Ian's. Although he was obviously older than her, he was by no means *old*, and he stirred something very primal in Sienna, something she'd never experienced before.

"Well?" Avery demanded.

"He's so good-looking," she whispered, unable to tear her gaze from the picture, those blue eyes startling and seemingly focused on her.

Avery laughed. "Someone is going to have a very good weekend."

"Hey, sugar, are you home?" Grey Kingston's distinct voice sounded from the other room.

"In the bedroom!" Avery called out. "Okay, my evening's about to start." She looked at Sienna. "And you need to get dressed for your date!"

Feeling herself blush, Sienna shook her head. "It's not a date! It's a school event," she said as much to remind her sister as to cement the fact in her own mind.

"With a private escort." Avery glanced over her shoulder as Grey's familiar face popped onto the screen.

"Hi, Sienna."

"Hey, Grey. We were just hanging up."

He grinned. "Always good to see you. But I wouldn't mind some time with my wife." He kissed Avery's cheek, and knowing what probably came next, Sienna called out, "Bye!" and disconnected the call.

She stared at her clothing, hoping her dress was

appropriate for tonight's event. She hadn't chosen something stifling and conservative because that wasn't who she was and the invitation had said semi-formal. But she hadn't picked something overly revealing, either. She wanted to come off suitable for the occasion.

With that thought in mind, she headed for the bathroom to wash up and dress for the evening, unable to get the image of her host for the night from her mind.

Want even more Carly books?

CARLY'S BOOKLIST by Series – visit:
http://smarturl.it/CarlyBooklist

Sign up for Carly's Newsletter:
http://smarturl.it/carlynews

Join Carly's Corner on Facebook:
facebook.com/groups/SerendipitysFinest

Carly on Facebook:
facebook.com/CarlyPhillipsFanPage

Carly on Instagram:
instagram.com/carlyphillips

Carly's Booklist

The Dare Series

Dare to Love Series
Book 1: Dare to Love (Ian & Riley)
Book 2: Dare to Desire (Alex & Madison)
Book 3: Dare to Touch (Dylan & Olivia)
Book 4: Dare to Hold (Scott & Meg)
Book 5: Dare to Rock (Avery & Grey)
Book 6: Dare to Take (Tyler & Ella)
A Very Dare Christmas – Short Story (Ian & Riley)

** Sienna Dare gets together with Ethan Knight in **The Knight Brothers** (Dare Me Tonight).*

** Jason Dare gets together with Faith in the **Sexy Series** (More Than Sexy).*

Dare NY Series (NY Dare Cousins)
Book 1: Dare to Surrender (Gabe & Isabelle)
Book 2: Dare to Submit (Decklan & Amanda)
Book 3: Dare to Seduce (Max & Lucy)

The Knight Brothers
Book 1: Take Me Again (Sebastian & Ashley)
Book 2: Take Me Down (Parker & Emily)
Book 3: Dare Me Tonight (Ethan Knight & Sienna Dare)
Novella: Take The Bride (Sierra & Ryder)
Take Me Now – Short Story (Harper & Matt)

The Sexy Series

Book 1: More Than Sexy (Jason Dare & Faith)

Book 2: Twice As Sexy (Landon & Vivienne)

Book 3: Better Than Sexy (Tanner & Scarlett)

Novella: Sexy Love (Shane & Amber)

Dare Nation

Book 1: Dare to Resist (Austin & Quinn)

Book 2: Dare to Tempt (Damon & Evie)

Book 3: Dare to Play (Jaxon & Macy)

Book 4: Dare to Stay (Brandon & Willow)

Novella: Dare to Tease (Hudson & Brianne)

* Paul Dare's sperm donor kids

Kingston Family

Book 1: Just One Night (Linc Kingston & Jordan Greene)

Book 2: Just One Scandal (Chloe Kingston & Beck Daniels)

Book 3: Just One Chance (Xander Kingston & Sasha Keaton)

Book 4: Just One Spark (Dash Kingston & Cassidy Forrester)

Book 5: Just One Wish (Axel Forrester)

Book 6: Just One Dare (Aurora Kingston & Nick Dare)

Other Indie Series

Billionaire Bad Boys
Book 1: Going Down Easy
Book 2: Going Down Hard
Book 3: Going Down Fast
Book 4: Going In Deep
Going Down Again – Short Story

Hot Heroes Series
Book 1: Touch You Now
Book 2: Hold You Now
Book 3: Need You Now
Book 4: Want You Now

Bodyguard Bad Boys
Book 1: Rock Me
Book 2: Tempt Me
Novella: His To Protect

Carly's Originally Traditionally Published Books

The Chandler Brothers
Book 1: The Bachelor
Book 2: The Playboy
Book 3: The Heartbreaker

Hot Zone

Book 1: Hot Stuff

Book 2: Hot Number

Book 3: Hot Item

Book 4: Hot Property

Costas Sisters

Book 1: Under the Boardwalk

Book 2: Summer of Love

Lucky Series

Book 1: Lucky Charm

Book 2: Lucky Break

Book 3: Lucky Streak

Bachelor Blogs

Book 1: Kiss Me if You Can

Book 2: Love Me If You Dare

Ty and Hunter

Book 1: Cross My Heart

Book 2: Sealed with a Kiss

Carly Classics (Unexpected Love)

Book 1: The Right Choice

Book 2: Perfect Partners

Book 3: Unexpected Chances

Book 4: Suddenly Love

Book 5: Worthy of Love

Carly Classics (The Simply Series)

Book 1: Simply Sinful

Book 2: Simply Scandalous

Book 3: Simply Sensual

Book 4: Body Heat (not currently available)

Book 5: Simply Sexy

* Every book stands alone – missing Body Heat won't hurt series enjoyment

Carly's Still Traditionally Published Books

Serendipity Series

Book 1: Serendipity*

Book 2: Destiny

Book 3: Karma

* May be difficult to find.

Serendipity's Finest Series

Book 1: Perfect Fling

Book 2: Perfect Fit

Book 3: Perfect Together

Serendipity Novellas

Book 1: Fated*

Book 2: Perfect Stranger*

* May be difficult to find.

Stand-Alone Books

Brazen

Secret Fantasy

Seduce Me

The Seduction

More Than Words Volume 7 – Compassion Can't Wait

Naughty Under the Mistletoe

Grey's Anatomy 101 Essay

About the Author

NY Times, Wall Street Journal, and USA Today Bestseller, Carly Phillips is the queen of Alpha Heroes, at least according to The Harlequin Junkie Reviewer. Carly married her college sweetheart and lives in Purchase, NY along with her crazy dogs who are featured on her Facebook and Instagram pages. The author of over 75 romance novels, she has raised two incredible daughters and is now an empty nester. Carly's book, The Bachelor, was chosen by Kelly Ripa as her first romance club pick. Carly loves social media and interacting with her readers. Want to keep up with Carly? Sign up for her newsletter and receive TWO FREE books at www.carlyphillips.com.

Made in United States
North Haven, CT
01 May 2024

51982647R00155